Spencer Hill Press

Contact: Spencer Hill Press, PO Box 247, Contoocook, NH 03229, USA

Please visit our website at www.spencerhillpress.com

First Edition November 2012.

Townsend, Angela J., 1969–
Amarok : a novel / by Angela J. Townsend – 1st edition
p. cm.
Summary:
A teenage girl in Alaska is abducted into the wilderness, where her only ally is a wolf that is more than what it seems.

Cover design by Carol D. Green.
Interior graphics by Angela J. Townsend.
Interior layout by Kate Kaynak.

The author acknowledges the trademarked status and trademark owners of the following wordmarks mentioned in this fiction: Dave and Busters, Disneyland, Earl Gray, iPod, Jell-O, Mercedes, Girl Scouts of America

ISBN 978-1-937053-22-2 (paperback)
ISBN 978-1-937053-23-9 (e-book)

Printed in the United States of America

Amarok

Angela J. Townsend

SPENCER HILL PRESS

To my family
and to
Milton Datsopoulos and Diane Larsen

You are the finest people I know

1

Friday, 3:30 a.m.
Attla, Alaska

Emma lifted the car keys from the hook on the wall, praying they wouldn't jingle as she crept across the kitchen floor. A floorboard creaked. She froze, peering down the dark hallway, her throat tight. Bedsprings squeaked, but her drunken stepfather didn't appear. Emma slipped on her parka, careful to slide the sleeves over the bruises on her arms, defensive wounds from Stan's fists. Most of the time her stepfather was careful not to leave any evidence of his abuse, but last night his cunning mind, the one he used in the courtroom as a prosecuting attorney, swam with booze. Emma searched for her snow boots, her gaze sweeping the floor. *Where were they?* A cough resonated from the master bedroom. Only a cough, but enough to send her heart racing.

Emma spotted her tennis shoes, shoved her feet into them, and bolted for the door. The knob rattled in her hand; she held her breath as she thrust the door open. Closing it quickly, Emma cringed, knowing it would creak, or bang, or make some kind of noise to give her away. But it shut without a sound. The porch light cut an icy path into the dark. Heavy snowflakes spiraled through the bitter cold air, melting on her face like tears.

Unsteady fingers jammed the key into the ignition of the Mercedes. It rumbled to life. Frozen leather seats crackled under her slight weight. She glanced at the kitchen door. Still closed, thank God. She flipped the defroster on high and backed out of the driveway. Catching a glimpse of herself in the rearview mirror, she hated what she saw.

How do you spell loser? E-M-M-A. Tears burned her eyes.

Soon, she'd be far away from snow and ice. Back to California, where they'd lived before her mother married Stan and they'd moved to Alaska. More tears. Happy memories hurled like knives, recalling the precious time before she'd caused her mother's death. Emma slammed the car into drive and accelerated down the narrow, twisty mountain road.

Snow mixed with rain fell in an endless river of white. She leaned over the steering wheel, straining to see beyond the hood ornament. Her wipers, on high speed, scraped violently over chunks of slush freezing on the windshield. Icy pellets hammered the roof of the car. The headlights reflected a swirling wall of mist.

Tension stiffened her neck. Emma swallowed hard, rotating her head for relief. The road curved into a glaring sheet of ice. The car fishtailed. Headlights swayed. She gripped the wheel in terror, turned into the skid, and regained control. Breathing a sigh of relief, Emma continued her descent, fingers tight on the wheel.

Her mouth suddenly went dry. Her purse—where was her purse? She shot a look into the passenger seat, then back at the road, and screamed.

2

Friday 3:45 a.m.

He couldn't remember the last time he had been alive—really alive. He faintly remembered a family—his mother, a raven-haired native, and his father, a French Canadian trapper. But that was a long time ago, a very long time. He'd stopped counting the years. Time didn't exist, only survival in the harsh Alaskan wilderness, with its sun-drenched summer nights and blinding winter snow.

As a wolf, he'd learned to gauge the seasons not only by the weather, but by events. The fall and winter months offered long, dark days with very little travel, except when his master poached the walrus for its iron-rich liver and ivory tusks. May brought pups to the ringed seals and fireweed to the tundra. July brought salmon to the rivers, and August produced abundant crops of tasty moss berries.

The thought of the ripe scarlet berries with their tart taste filled his senses and his mind wandered back to the preserves his mother had made—the thick, sweet jam that'd held them over for the winter and the gooey pot he would lick clean after it cooled. He could still hear her calling from the door of their home. Calling his name… what was it? He thought hard. As the fog in his mind cleared, it came to him, his mother's warm voice, light with bright summer laughter… Tok… his name had been Tok. There might have been more but her voice faded, swallowed by the fog once again.

He had no trouble remembering his death, though, a painful battle to the end. Nor would Tok forget the old native who'd arrived at his bedside, leaning over him, chanting in an ancient tongue, rattling and shaking caribou bones, denying him the peace that true death brings. Hours later, he'd woken in the old man's hut lying on his back, staring at a roof made of whale ribs and seal skins.

Tok rolled onto his side, writhing in a sudden burst of pain. His bones elongated, converging with muscle and fur. His jaw stretched and twisted as his teeth forced their way through torn, bleeding gums. Tok tried to shout as the agony wracked his seventeen-year-old body, but the sound tightened in his throat, taking his screams and warping his pain, transforming his cry into a sorrowful howl. His hands tore at his misshapen head, and claws split through the tender skin where fingers and toes had been.

Over the next hour, Tok's hearing and sense of smell increased. With every gust of wind his wolf heart raced, smelling the lemmings nesting between the logs of the cabin. This repulsed and frightened him. His senses grew even more acute as days went on. As his instincts sharpened, he became more frightened of the old shaman—a cold, soulless creature, whose loathsome touch singed Tok's nerves. When he was able to stand, a man by the name of Ryan purchased him, and he never saw the native again.

Now, many years later, he traveled through the early dawn. More wolf than human, he hunted with his cruel captor—a descendant of the first brutal man who'd enslaved him. Years ago, he'd given up on finding the totems that would free him. When the time was right, he'd rip out his master's throat and will himself to turn to dust, as he should have long ago. Death would be his freedom.

A bitter sorrow stirred inside him. He would miss the tundra almost as much as he missed being a man, and he would miss watching over herds of musk oxen while his master harvested their wool. He would also miss hunting caribou, the gurgling rivers packed with ice floes, and the northern lights coloring the frozen prairie in vivid hues of scarlet.

Maybe he wasn't ready to die—not yet.

3

Friday, 4:00 a.m.

A bull moose stood in the center of the highway. Emma stomped on the brakes, immediately realizing her mistake. Never hit the skids on ice. Shit—too late. The Mercedes skewed sideways. She caught the wheel, turning into the spin. The vehicle whipped around and around, left the road and reeled over an embankment. Tree limbs twisted and snapped as the car plowed through their frozen arms, crashing down the steep mountainside. Emma stood on the brakes, clutching the steering wheel until her fingers went numb. She bit her lower lip, tasted blood, and wondered if this was the same insane fear her mother had endured when her car plunged into the frozen river.

The Mercedes slammed to a halt in a thick grove of pine trees. The seatbelt gripped hard as Emma jolted forward. Air bags exploded like sprouting mushrooms. A white dust filled the air. Choking on the powder, Emma's mind filled with images of her dead mother drowning in the icy river, dragged down into the frozen blackness. Panic cut into her veins, sawing at her last nerve. She yanked on the door handle. It opened a crack, stopping hard against the base of a towering pine. Emma slammed the door over and over into the trunk of the tree. She couldn't breathe—she had to get out.

She fumbled for the controls, hit the right button, and the window rolled down. Frigid air swirled inside. Emma gulped down a precious lungful and struggled to escape the mangled car.

In the distance, icy granules crunched under lumbering footsteps.

"Help!"

The crunching drew near, heavy and uneven.

"Please, help me!"

A sinister cackle echoed in the belly of the night.

The car's headlights winked and faded out. Engulfed in darkness, Emma scrambled to roll the window up. It wouldn't budge. *No, not now!*

"Hello?"

Footsteps sounded at her side.

"Is someone there?"

Silence.

A heavy scent of booze polluted the air, astringent in her nostrils. Emma froze, her ears attuned to every sound.

A voice, low and threatening, carried on the wind. "I can smell your fear."

She started to disconnect, to spiral away, to disappear from this moment where danger lurked.

"I can hear your heart beating."

Emma's head jerked up. A dark face hovered over her, like the moon's evil twin.

A wooden club flashed.

The world exploded in brilliant pinpricks of light.

4

Friday, 5:00 a.m.

Three winters had passed since his master had last taken a victim. The memory of her blood sang in his head and, unconsciously, he salivated. By the time they'd reached the cabin, her icy flesh had bled no more. Tok cringed, remembering his master's anger at her death, and the beating he'd suffered for it.

The woman's disappearance had brought strangers into the woods, men with badges and guns. He remembered the gunshots on the day he'd gotten too close, and the strange smells of oil and smoke which lingered in the air long after they'd gone. He recalled the night sky lit with flashing lights and flying machines, but the forest and snow had hidden him and his master well, and eventually the strangers had left and never returned. His enslaver had bided his time, waiting patiently until now to risk another kidnapping. Finding a woman alone and trapped in the woods provided the perfect opportunity.

Tok wanted to stop him, to lash out and tear him with his sharp fangs, but he knew it would do little good. Somewhere, hidden carefully away, the Ryan family possessed the totem that controlled him.

This particular master was much worse than the last. Young, resentful, and cruel, with a seething hatred for anyone he encountered on the trail. His nickname—Weasel Tail—came from the vermin tassels that decorated his sealskin boots, and it suited him well.

Tok sat on a frost heave, watching his master pull the young girl from the car. He'd need his rest for the long trip through the woods and up the steep mountain to the hateful place he called home. His stomach ached; he hadn't eaten in two days. Thankfully, more snow would follow and slow the caribou. Hunting alone—without a pack to wear down his prey—was difficult. Maybe he'd sniff out a rabbit in a mossy den, or a juicy ptarmigan nesting in the snow.

Metal squealed and Tok's scoop-like ears swiveled. Weasel Tail wrenched open the passenger side door and lifted the girl from the wreckage. Her arms dangled at her sides. Long thick hair, red as moss berries, swung below her shoulders. Her chin tilted upward. The moon peeked from behind the clouds and illuminated her smooth jaw line. She appeared young and thin. This worried him; if she wasn't strong, she'd never survive. Had she been badly wounded in the crash? Perhaps not—he would've smelled more blood. His sensitive nose could detect it even a couple of miles away. The presence of the moon and the autumnal bite of the wind soothed his concern. That meant it was still early fall, though snow tumbled from the sky.

The past few nights, stars had shone with uncommon brilliance, a phenomenon that often meant the bitter north wind would bring winter whipping at their backs. With shorter days and colder nights, he'd noticed changes within the forest creatures, animals and plants preparing for a long, hard season. Squirrels chattered while they cut pinecones and stashed them in grass-lined caches, flocks of birds left for warmer climates and the plants of the tundra were already turning dormant. Maybe they'd have time to get the girl to shelter before it was too late.

Tok rose to his feet, sniffing at her long limp fingers, memorizing her scent. She smelled pleasant, like the cotton grass blooming across the tundra in the spring—lush nourishment for snow geese and caribou calves, a healing substance to soothe his aching belly when he chewed the mineral-rich stems.

Like all wolves, Tok could see in dim light, and what he saw made him uneasy. He didn't like the way Weasel Tail eyed the girl. Tok peered into the ice fog. He remembered a cabin somewhere in this area, possibly just a few yards ahead. Maybe if he made enough noise, someone would come for her and interrupt his master's terrible plan. He lowered his haunches, threw back his head and howled. His gully-deep voice resonated through the arctic dawn.

A hard boot to his ribs quickly shut him up. Pain seared into Tok's chest. He whirled to sink his teeth into the man's thigh, but his oxygen-starved lungs made him gasp for air instead. Weasel Tail growled, heaved the young girl up on his wide shoulder, and headed into the dark. Tok held his muzzle low and trotted to catch up, ignoring the burn in his ribcage. He didn't want to lose sight of the girl. Maybe he could protect her—unlike the last one, who had died so quickly.

A polar wind blew across his ruff, carrying a musky scent that made him pause. He opened his jaws slightly, lifted his nose and tasted the air.

Needles of fear prickled his spine.
Danger.

5

Friday, 6:00 a.m.

A blinding throb hammered Emma's temples. She couldn't open her eyes—not yet—easier to slip back into the haze. But as she sank into a sea of unconsciousness, her mother's pale face rose from the murky depths, hands plastered against the driver's side window, mouth open, eyes wide with fright. The air squeezed from Emma's lungs. She let the water slide down her throat, drowning in the same river that'd cradled her mother in its chilly embrace. This was the price she deserved to pay for causing her mother's death.

She jolted awake, gasping for breath. A chill stabbed deep into her bones like an ice pick. Someone carried her slung over a shoulder with a viselike grip on her legs. *Where am I?* She opened her mouth to speak, struggling to regain full consciousness. *Fight! Kick! Do something!* Cloaked figures slipped past. *Who are they? What do they want?* The blur in her eyes cleared and she saw the dark figures were trees.

How had she gotten here? Images flickered through her mind. The icy roads. The moose. The blurry outline of the steering wheel and the white glare of snow pressed against her headlights. She'd heard the crunch of footsteps and then someone, *something*, had hit her, until darkness swallowed all. Was it Stan? No it couldn't be Stan, he'd be too drunk to carry her anywhere and he'd never beaten her unconscious—he'd never dared. She'd always fought back with such fury, biting, clawing, kicking—whatever it took to get him off her. Adrenaline coursed through her veins, sending a rush of blood throbbing into her ears. Emma lifted her head, the pain of the movement threatening to bring the darkness again. She kicked and pounded her fists on the wide back until the abductor slammed her to the ground in a heap.

A pair of buckskin-clad legs straddled her, cutting off any chance of escape. A man's face, partially concealed behind a heavy hood, leaned in close.

"Who are you?" Emma demanded. "What do you want?"

He seized her bruised wrist, pain flashed, and a scream ripped from Emma's throat. He drew back and slapped her hard, bringing tears to her eyes.

"Shut up!" he growled. "You're hurtin' my ears."

The hood made of animal skins fell away and cold, dark eyes penetrated hers. Emma searched his rugged features, her face stinging from the slap. *Who is he?* A thick scar ran the entire length of one cheek and disappeared into a scruffy beard.

The dirt-caked edges of his mouth stretched into a sly smile. "You can fuss all you want. Ain't nobody gonna save you."

Emma wormed her way from between his legs, scrambling to her feet. Her shattered mind raced. *Run! Move!* She bolted for the tree line, but he lashed out, catching her ankle. She fell to the ground, frozen pine needles poking into her palms as she scrabbled upright. He grabbed her parka, hauled her backward, and caught her around the waist. Emma jabbed with her elbow, connecting with his throat. Wheezing, he smashed his fist into her side. Emma stopped struggling, mouth open, gasping for air. Waves of pain, as sharp and stunning as a blade through the ribs, stabbed at her insides. She couldn't think, couldn't move, couldn't breathe, until the darkness washed over her.

Finally. Thank God. She would die.

Snatching her clear up off her feet, he shook her hard, forcing her back from the darkness. He whirled her around, clamping his arms around her. She sucked in what air she could, forcing her suffering limbs to move, kicking, punching, and twisting to be free, fighting with everything she had. He held her easily with one arm, whipped out a knife, and pressed it against her throat. The cold blade kissed her skin as he leaned in, growling in her ear. "Try running again and I'll slice your ankles. Got it?"

She clutched her ribs and nodded, her vision blurry, her mind reeling. He pushed her away with a disgusted grunt and narrowed his gaze into the trees, scowling. He slipped two grimy fingertips into his mouth and let out a low whistle.

Emma caught vapor-like glimpses of a huge wolf weaving between trees and shrubs. The creature's fur shone like sterling silver against a fresh layer of snowfall. A large leather pack burdened its back as it burst from the brush. The muscular rhythms in the wolf's powerful neck and shoulders made its movements appear almost effortless. The creature circled, moving in closer, glaring at her with ferocious yellow eyes. Emma stared at the predator, her pulse quickening. Although it belonged to the man, the animal appeared wild, and she realized the weight of the stranger's threat. If he didn't slice her ankles, this creature was certainly capable of doing it, and any glimmer of hope she might've held withered under the harsh amber glare.

For a second the wolf's eyes seemed to soften, transforming into an almost human expression, and in that instant Emma recognized something she knew all too well—a sadness so deep, a wound so painful, it was unreachable, untreatable, hopeless.

The expression left the creature's eyes almost before it registered, and she wondered if she'd imagined it in her desperate need of a friend. Hesitantly, she reached out her hand. The wolf leapt back in surprise, lips retracting into a snarl.

Emma stared at the animal's fangs. Her blood turned to ice. The wolf lowered its muzzle, stalking closer, the ruff on its neck rising. Emma swayed, her vision fading again. She closed her eyes and pressed her fingers into her temples, slipping away, disappearing inside her own skin. *No, not now, Em. Come on!* She had a bad habit of losing it in stressful situations—disconnecting from the world when things got tough. It'd started the night her mother died, when the coroner had given her the terrible news. Blood had rushed in her ears and she'd felt herself floating away, giving in to the blessed relief from the shock and pain. Better to drift away than to stay and endure such overwhelming grief. It was happening more and more often these days, making her fear that one day she might drift too far and never return. Better to be dead than a nut job. *Come on! Snap out of it!*

Emma rubbed her face with her freezing hands, forcing herself back into reality. She narrowed her eyes at the man. "What are you going to do to me?"

"Never mind! Do what I say, or I'll kill you."

For some strange reason, this struck her as funny and she started to giggle, tears streaming down her face. She always laughed when she was nervous, but never like this. She laughed out loud, uncontrollably. The poor, stupid bastard had managed to kidnap the only teenager in the world who didn't give a shit whether she lived or died. And what was he going to do? Hold her for ransom? Who would pay for her safe return? No one. And for some reason, that made her laugh even harder. Then the laughter turned to sorrow, laced with fear. She'd screwed up everyone and everything she'd ever cared about. She deserved this.

The man scowled. "What's so funny?"

Emma crossed her arms and turned her back on him.

"I asked you a question!"

Emma ignored him, biting the inside of her cheek.

An autumn wind whistled past, sending skeletal leaves and brittle pine needles skittering across the snow. Emma heard his heavy footsteps crunching behind her. She closed her eyes and gritted her teeth, bracing herself.

He grabbed her by the hair and yanked her head back. "Answer me!"

Anger blistered her soul. Emma knotted her fists, spread her feet shoulder-width apart, and lashed out, kicking him hard in the knee.

"Shit!" He stumbled but recovered quickly, grabbing her from behind and pinning her arms at her sides. His sinewy body emanated a blazing heat that burned into her back like a brand. The stench of him turned her stomach, the smell increasing with every desperate flare of her nostrils. He leaned in closer, his rancid breath feathering her neck.

"Let go of me!"

"Not until you answer me!" he growled.

Emma clamped her lips tighter and he increased his grip, crushing her until she saw flashes of light dancing before her eyes. An intense drumming rushed into her ears and she realized that it was the frantic pounding of blood in her veins. Emma stopped struggling. She'd let go and die so she could be with her mother—tell her how much she loved her, how sorry she was for everything that'd happened. He loosened his grasp, and instinctively her lungs filled with life-giving air.

He burrowed his nose into her hair, sniffing like an animal, running his crusty lips along the base of her neck. "Mmmm, you smell good."

He flicked his snake-like tongue around her ear and shoved a hand inside her coat as she lay trapped in his arms. Despite her weakness, she tried to punch and kick to get away but it did little good as the hammering in her head intensified. He could do whatever he wanted to her dead body. She'd be long gone, to a place where no one could hurt her. Flashes of light and darkness danced before her eyes and then she spotted the wolf, advancing. It crouched and then jumped through the air, sinking his fangs into the man's arm.

The man let go of her and spun around, trying to free himself from the attack. He tripped and landed hard on his back beneath the enraged wolf. The creature released his arm and snapped at the man's face in a fury, inches from tearing him apart. The man knocked the creature to one side, reaching inside his shirt to pull out an ivory object on a leather cord. The wolf hesitated, curling its lips in an angry snarl, then slunk away into the cover of the trees.

The man got to his feet scowling at her. "What are you looking at?"

Emma turned away, shivering. She couldn't bear the thought of him touching her again, and if he really wanted her dead, why hadn't he already killed her? Why bother to pack her through the woods into the middle of nowhere? Her shoulders sagged.

Maybe death wouldn't come as quickly as she'd hoped. Or as painlessly, for that matter. The frosty air burned her eyes, and tears froze to her face, stinging her cheeks.

She scanned the area for an escape route, watching the first golden glow of dawn peek over the snow-girdled mountains. Nothing looked familiar. How had they covered so much ground since last night, and in the dark? There'd be no roads. No landmarks. Her heart sank. No one to help her for miles. She'd welcomed death, but this wasn't how she wanted it to end. Emma longed to see the sandy coastlines of California just once more before she died, and to see her friends. Guilt tugged at her heart. Emma knew her mother would've wanted her to survive. But her mother was dead—why should she be allowed to live when the accident had been her fault?

A flash of movement turned her attention to the wolf. For some reason the creature had saved her, and she was grateful. The wolf glared at her, its eyes full of mistrust. For the first time in a very long while, Emma felt something beside grief and despair. She felt empathy for another living, breathing life form. Before her mother's death, before she was numb, she'd loved animals, especially huskies with their brilliant blue eyes and endless stamina. But this was no dog. This was a wild creature. Maybe not a purebred, as he looked different from the wolves she had seen in the wildlife museum in Wilsu, and even though he'd growled at her, she pitied the poor beast. The huge backpack he carried looked much too heavy for his frame. Judging by his temperament and his snapping response to her hand, he'd never known kindness. He seemed as miserable as she was, if not more so.

The kidnapper reached inside the folds of his fur-lined coat, pulled out a sinewy string of dried meat, and dangled it in front of the wolf's nose. The wolf licked his muzzle and whined. The man jerked forward, stomping one foot as if to chase the beast, and the wolf recoiled. He grinned, watching the creature slink away. Fury branded Emma's soul. How could anyone treat an animal so poorly?

The man scowled and tore the jerky in half. He handed Emma a piece. Her skin crawled at the greasy feel of the meat and the fragments of gristle still attached. The pungent odor of the dried flesh made her stomach churn and she knew she wouldn't be able to keep it down.

Emma eyed the hungry wolf. Although muscular in the shoulders, she could count his clearly defined ribs. She pitied the poor animal, so alone, without anyone to care for him. Such a familiar feeling. Since her mother's death, loneliness had leached the happiness from her bones, leaving only anger and sorrow battling inside of her. A lone wolf herself, she was every inch of five feet tall and barely weighed a hundred pounds. What she lacked in size, she made up in bravery. A thrill-seeker and storyteller, Emma wove tales of great danger to impress her friends—stories drummed up at the last minute to explain the scars lining her arms.

Emma swallowed hard. No story she'd ever told could match the truth of what was happening to her now.

The man turned his back, and Emma tossed the meat near the wolf. The animal crept closer, his head turned partly away in distrust. He paused, his cold, yellow eyes peering sideways at her, and then lowered his muzzle, noisily snapping up the offering.

The man spun around, lips tight with anger. He closed the space between them with big earth-eating strides. "How do you expect him to hunt for your dinner if he ain't hungry?"

Before Emma could answer he snatched the front of her parka and shook her hard. Pain slashed into her neck, jarring her spine. She tried to pull away, but he jerked her even closer, inches from his face, his breath reeking of booze. "You just mind your own business, or I'll shut you up for good."

Emma pulled back. "Get your hands off me!"

He released her, cursing under his breath as he hiked to a nearby rock and sat with a heavy grunt. He cut his eyes at her. "How old are you? Sixteen? Seventeen?"

"Seventy-four!" she snapped. "What do you care?"

"Just wondering," he said with a mouth full of jerky. "You might not get any older if you don't watch that smart mouth of yours."

"Why? What are you gonna do to me?"

He ignored her, chewing louder, raising his eyes to the frost-heavy wind.

Maybe this was the wrong approach. Maybe if she was nicer to him, she could get him to trust her, fool him into thinking she was his friend. When she was strong enough and the haze in her head cleared, she'd make a run for it.

Emma forced a smile, brushing the snow from her pants. "It must be hard for you living out here in the woods alone." A stupid thing to say, but she couldn't think of anything else.

He shrugged and narrowed his piggy eyes. Maybe he wasn't as stupid as he looked. His gaze slipped from her face, traveling down her body. Emma's skin grew even colder.

Maybe being friendly was a bad idea.

6

Tok stood on the brow of a hill and scanned the vast wilderness below him, trying to quell his sense of unease. Thankfully, he'd been able to fend off Weasel Tail's attack on the girl and he'd continue to do so as long as his strength held out. He took a few short sniffs of the northern wind. The alarming scent he'd detected earlier had faded into the breeze. His eyes shifted to the girl. Tok hadn't meant to snarl at her, to scare her. She'd surprised him by reaching out. He hadn't been shown kindness in years, and his wolf instincts remained strong, along with the raw, unrelenting hunger burning in his belly.

He worked his way down the hill, pausing at the scent of arctic willow. His wolf heart quickened. The crisp leaves provided a tasty meal for caribou migrating to their winter quarters. Tok listened for the clicking sounds of tendons slipping over bones in their hooves as they walked. His mouth watered. Maybe he could find a weak one, take it down without a hard fight, and feast on its juicy flesh.

Tok crested another rise in the landscape, wondering how much humanity he retained, and if someday it would disappear completely. It frightened him to think how much of himself he'd already lost. The memories of his parents came and went. Some days, when the blood sang in him, he could hardly remember being a man, and now the first act of kindness he'd received in many years he'd repaid with a snap of his jaws. He desperately wished he could tell her how sorry he was, but words were denied him now.

Tok scanned the lonesome terrain for prey. Nothing. Not even a lemming. He scratched at the frosty earth, circled a few times, and settled down. The afternoon sky vaulted above him in shades of gray, adding to his gloom. Gnawing on the ice that had collected between his toes, he fought to remember more of his past. Memories, deep and chilling as the Bering Sea, washed over him.

The summer he turned seventeen, his family followed the lure of the gold rush from Canada to Alaska. Tok's father had marveled at their good fortune to settle in such a pristine valley, near clear, cool, running water. Natives warned them to stay away. The land wasn't safe. For centuries, every creature that came near had died or disappeared.

The last day Tok spent with his father, they walked the trap lines, checking all of their favorite spots. Father stood in the summer sun, pushed back his beaver-skin cap and smiled, pleased with their catch and proud of his son's work. His father spoke of a rich future, on this fertile land. They'd come in sight of their cabin as the sun sank over the mountaintops when they spotted the old native—neither Inupiat nor Yupik, but from some unknown tribe—standing in the distance. Just standing, and staring. Father waved and called to the old man to come closer if he wished.

Few natives ever passed this way. They did not like to enter this valley and spoke in hushed whispers of curses and crooked spirits. The few who did would trade what they had or sometimes, when the harsh winter was at its worst, beg for scraps of food. Tok's father always spared what they could, when they could, and in return the natives offered spells of protection. This land made them uneasy, they explained. It wasn't safe. But for all his kind heart, Tok's father was a proud man; he wouldn't let the land beat him, or let himself be driven away by superstition. Tok would often find carved sticks and bones by the front of his house, totems left by the natives to ward off dark spirits. Tok's father would laugh and throw them on the fire. "We have no need of charms," he would say. "God protects."

A chill penetrated Tok's spine as the old man stood and stared, not acknowledging his father or his offer. Later that night, the flicker of a campfire blazed in the distance. Tok swore he could hear a quiet moaning, but his father frowned and blamed it on the wind. Tok went to bed with a troubled feeling. He woke to the sounds of vomiting.

Father brushed off their concern for his health, claiming time would heal him. Tok's mother fed him warm bread and broth, but everything his father ate came up again. The day wore on and his father grew paler, sitting in front of the hearth, shivering despite the roaring blaze. Tok kept the fire high, trying to fight his father's illness with sweat and hard work.

Father groaned and complained about the fuss, insisting he had work to do and he needed to shake this sickness before nighttime or it would be too dark to check the snares. Tok went in his place. By the time he returned, darkness coated the land.

Tok stood on the porch before entering the cabin. The campfire still flickered in the same place it had the night before. He opened the cabin door greeted by the sweltering heat of a furnace, yet his father still sat in front of the fire and shivered. His mother stood next to her husband, holding his hand, the tears drying on her cheeks in the heat. Father stared into the fireplace, incoherent mumbling the only sign he still clung on. Tok knew then that the old native somehow, God only knows how, had something to do with this. He took a rifle from its place over the mantle and rummaged in the great shoulder bag his father took with him on their walks. Tok's hands closed over the bullets. He threw the door open and rushed outside.

His fear for his father's health brought tears that blurred his sight, but he didn't care. He hiked to the fire and pointed the weapon at the old native's chest, but his shot went high and wide. And in that one act, something changed. Like the snapping of elastic stretched too tight, something was different. Then he heard his mother cry out, and he ran back to the cabin to find his father slumped forward in the chair, a last thread of saliva running down to the quilt in which he was wrapped.

Tok's mother buried her head in her husband's chest and cried, great sobs wracking her soul, until Tok lifted her firmly and took her over to the bed. She was too exhausted to struggle and lay weak and pale on the coverlet of furs. Tok wrapped his father gently in the blanket, and then took a large needle and thread and sewed it closed. He would bury the body in the morning.

Tok sat in his father's chair until sleep claimed him, still cradling the rifle. He woke to the sound of his mother vomiting, and a cold, clammy hand took his heart. The rest of the day he dug through the permafrost, making a hole deep enough to bury his father, then piled on enough rocks and stones to stop the animals from feasting on his remains.

When he finished, he trudged into the cabin to find his mother shivering at the fire, face pale and blank. Too tired to even cry, Tok turned around and went back outside. He began to dig a second hole alongside the first.

The next morning he stood, silently whispering a brief prayer over both graves. Tok's heart nearly burst as he stabbed wooden crosses into the earth as grave markers. Then a wave of cramps hit his stomach, and the sickness overtook him as well.

Tok barely clung to life, with his mind fevered and his throat so tight he could hardly breathe. He lay for a week in his bunk, only able to swallow a few sips of water. Then the old native arrived.

Too weak to save himself, he lay helpless while his body painfully morphed from man to beast. Harder times came later, when he struggled to adjust to being a wolf, unable to accept what he had become. Unable to cry or speak, only to whine and howl like a depraved beast.

Tok had looked at the old man with questioning eyes. Why? Why had he done this to him? The native glared as if reading Tok's mind, and then told him the story of his people, mammoth hunters who'd lived during the ice age. He was the great Milak, a shaman of the Kuno tribe. They'd experienced a winter like no other, and provisions ran low. The earth turned to endless sheets of ice, and storms raked over the land like the claws of a saber-tooth tiger.

With the coming of the howling winds and endless snow, his hunting songs failed to bring the gift of the mammoth to the hunters of the tribe. Many moons passed, and still no mammoths came. The small band feared the great spirits no longer heard Milak's songs, so they abandoned him. Angry and resentful, Milak turned to the dark spirits of the land to give him revenge on his tribe and all who entered this valley.

Milak found refuge in a cave, and he sat near the lip overlooking the deep valley, chanting to the crooked spirits to make his old body immortal. In return, he promised to do their bidding for all time. He cursed the valley so his small band of people could never return, and to doom all others who dared to enter. The dark spirits taught him to change the forms of living things, to enslave them in new bodies and draw magical strength from the transformation. The old shaman slept for centuries, impervious to the cold or to hunger, and woke when the frozen tundra had thawed and daylight spilled across the land. He'd paused then, staring at Tok, a sinister grin of satisfaction spreading across his leathery face.

Tok shut his eyes, forcing out the painful memory.

He wondered how many others were like him, trapped in the bodies of animals. He only knew of one other—one whom the darkness had nearly consumed—and for two days he'd smelled Suka's terrifying scent. The creature, once a man, stood on the edge of madness, and Tok couldn't blame him. To know there was no hope of release was to invite despair. And when the form of the prison comes with tooth and claw then despair and madness can turn to hate, a hatred so strong it yearns to savage the world in an avalanche of blood and death.

For the girl's sake, Tok prayed they wouldn't cross Suka's path.

7

"Take off that parka."

Emma flayed him with her eyes. "No way!"

He stepped toward her, teeth clenched. "I said, take it off!"

Emma hesitated. He wrapped his grimy fingers around an ivory knife handle on his belt. A muscle near his eye twitched, and he drew out a long, thin blade. Emma glared at the weapon. She'd never backed down from anyone, not even Stan when he'd threatened to slice her with a broken wine bottle or the time he'd gotten drunk and aimed a forty-five at her eye. But this man was different; there was something evil about him, inhuman. He enjoyed hurting rather than killing, like a cat toying with an injured bird.

"Fine!" She tore off the coat, flung it at his feet, and planted her hands on her hips.

He pinned her with his eyes, hatred burning in his stare. He sheathed the knife and snatched the jacket.

Emma shivered in the bitter cold. "So is this your brilliant plan, genius? To freeze me to death?"

He raised his hand to slap her, but his eyes darted to her arms. A wicked smile curled the corners of his thin lips. "Where'd you get all those scars?"

She turned away, wrapping her arms around herself. Unexpected tears filled Emma's eyes, and that made her even madder. She didn't want to cry, and she didn't want to discuss her scars with this creep.

"What's the matter? You gonna cry?" He threw his head back and laughed. "Little spoiled brat wants her mommy? Whaaaaaaaaaa!"

"Shut up!"

He muttered under his breath and stalked off, stuffing the coat into his backpack.

Emma glared at him, wishing she could make him pay—grab the knife from his belt and sink it deep into his chest, laughing in his ugly face as the blood drained from his worthless, stinking body. She pressed the heels of her hands against her eyes. She wouldn't let him get to her. That's what he wanted. She could see it in his eyes. He thrived on pain and misery.

Rage burned inside her like lit gasoline. She sucked in a deep breath, slowing her heartbeat and embracing the anger. Anger was her friend. Anger was a good thing, because when she was mad she couldn't disconnect. She couldn't drift away. And drifting away was the last thing she needed right now.

Footsteps padded beside her and something wet and warm slithered across her skin. Her eyelids flew open. She jerked her arm away and peered into the soft, yellow eyes of the wolf. He had licked her, felt sorry for her. With that one act of sheer kindness she started to cry.

"Get back!" the man yelled. He kicked at the wolf and missed. "No, don't! He didn't do anything."

The wolf's eyes turned cold. He growled, flattening his ears to his head and bristling his fur. The man stomped forward, trying for another kick. The creature lowered its muzzle, trotted to the top of a frost heave, and glanced back at Emma before disappearing into a dip in the landscape.

An aura of hopelessness strangled her soul, like a dark mist that wouldn't rise. She hated to see the wolf go—dejected, miserable, alone—just like her. Her life was like a freight train that had jumped the tracks. How had everything gone so terribly wrong? Gotten so out of control? All she could do was fight, because that's all she had left. She'd always been strong, always been a rebel, but now the sorrow she carried weighed so heavily on her shoulders it threatened to extinguish the basic urge to survive.

The man grabbed his backpack, rummaged around, and jerked out a dirty fur coat. He scowled, tossing it at Emma's feet. Freezing, she picked it up, examined it, and wrinkled her nose. It reeked of wood smoke, but all she really cared about at that moment was covering her arms. She couldn't bear to look at her own scars or the bruises from Stan, each one a raw reminder of how she'd failed. Her anger and sorrow united, and then she went numb. Why did she have to hash over all of this now? And why did painful memories have to haunt her when she didn't want to face them?

None of it made any sense because, in the beginning, she'd done all the right things. She'd gone to the school counselor, but he'd betrayed her, telling her mother she'd been cutting herself. Emma had trusted him not to tell. She'd gone to him in a fury, demanding to know why he'd told on her. All he could do was stand there in his stupid polyester suit and show her the sections in the student handbook that stated the reasons why. He was worried about her. It was his duty. He was obligated by law to tell. Blah. Blah. Blah. She understood the reasons, but it left her with no one to confide in. She'd cried herself to sleep, abandoned and miserable. Who could she trust now? No one. So she'd learned to keep her mouth shut, to just smile and say everything was fine.

Her mother had confronted her, yelling and threatening to send her to an institution if she cut herself again. Emma couldn't bear the thought of it. She'd be so far behind in school, and her friends would think she was crazy. She'd been in a hospital before, when her drinking had gotten out of control. She'd hated it there. It was like being in a prison. Why had she done this to herself? Why did she do things that ruined her life? Why didn't she just stop?

Emma wished she had all the answers, but what else could she have done? Cutting had been her only form of relief from all the pain for the past two years, since her mother had met that asshole, Stan. She'd felt caged and closed in, and she'd had to release it. If she hadn't cut herself, how could she have taken the pain?

Emma knew she'd hurt her mother. She knew she'd disappointed her. And that brought more pain... and that made her want to reach for the razor again. Her mother had wanted them to be one big happy family, for life to be perfect. But Emma wasn't happy, and her life was far from perfect. Why couldn't her mother have just held her and told her everything would be all right instead of yelling at her, accusing her of destroying her life with Stan? Why couldn't she understand that this was the only way Emma knew to cope with all the pain? Losing her friends, traveling hundreds of miles into the middle of nowhere, and rejection from a father she'd never known.

Now her mother was dead. There'd be no making up for what had happened that night. No apologies, no relief from the guilt.

Emma watched as the man zipped up the pack and secured it on his back. He whistled, and the wolf trotted over the rise. The animal drew near, all the while keeping his eyes on Emma. He paused a few feet away, stiff-legged and tall, ears erect and forward. She wanted desperately to stroke his head, to return the kindness he had shown her—to prove that not all humans were bad. Maybe the wolf would turn on his abusive master and rip his throat out. Emma could only hope.

The man knelt beside the wolf, reaching for the pack on its back. The animal rolled his ears tightly against his head, snarling and gnashing at the man's face. He snatched the wolf by the hide of his neck and punched the animal in the head. The wolf sank his teeth into the man's forearm. The man struck the creature again and again, until the wolf went limp and started to whimper. He hurled the wolf to the ground, lifting a boot to crush his skull.

"No, don't!"

The man stopped, whirling around. He flashed a smug grin. "What's the matter? You feel sorry for this pile of fur?"

"Just leave him alone."

"Why? Bet he wouldn't feel a thing for you, if I cut out that bleeding heart of yours."

"I don't care. He's only doing what comes naturally. When you abuse him, how do you expect him to react?"

He snorted and knelt beside the wolf, opened the knapsack and pulled out a pair of snow boots. "Put 'em on," he ordered. "They'll keep your feet warm. Don't want to pack ya if your damn toes freeze."

He hurled them at her, but she ducked and they flopped behind her. An arctic wind whipped through the trees, howling over the land. Emma shuddered at the haunting sound as her scalp pulled tight. She quickly slipped off her shoes and slid the boots on. The short exposure to the chilly weather made the frozen soles of her feet burn. The boots were definitely a lot warmer.

"Thanks."

He hacked and spit on the ground. "Don't thank me. I didn't do it for you. Now give me those stupid girly shoes. I don't want search dogs sniffing you out."

Emma snorted. Search dogs? What a joke. No one would come looking for her. She had no one except Stan, and all he cared about were his stupid car and getting drunk. Anger pulsed in her veins, remembering how the drunken pig had told her to get out just days after her mother had died. He hadn't even given her a chance to grieve. All he could think of was his own loss, but she almost couldn't blame him. She'd been responsible for all that had happened.

Funny thing is, she would've gladly gone, but Stan refused to pay for her flight to Los Angeles, even though he made big bucks as an attorney. He just wanted her gone, and expected her to leave with nothing. The only way out was to jack Stan's car. Problem was, as much as he wanted her to leave, he didn't want to lose his precious Mercedes and had hidden the keys. Last night he'd been too drunk to hide them or notice anything and she had made her escape… or so she'd thought. Some escape. All that trouble and here she was, kidnapped by a crazy dirt bag.

It was all so unfair. She gritted her teeth and flung her shoes at the man. One hit his left shoulder. He narrowed his eyes. *Take that, creep!* She wriggled her toes inside the oversized boots. Although warm, she'd never be able to run in them. Maybe this was part of his plan, to keep her from escaping. He snarled and thrust his hands into a pair of moose-skin gloves. Emma narrowed her eyes at him, searching for a weak point. She'd do anything to run his own blade across his throat. Cut *him* until he bled. Take out all her anger and problems on this asshole who'd dared to kidnap her.

She studied his face. His skin, although finely lined from sun and chapped from the wind, wasn't as rugged as she thought, and his beard wasn't speckled with gray. It was the first time she'd realized how young he was. His rustic appearance had fooled her.

"You don't look that much older than me. You sure you know what you're doing?"

"What do you mean?" he snapped.

"Just wondering why someone so young would throw their life away kidnapping a girl and going to jail. You must have a good reason. I won't press charges if you take me back now."

He lurched forward and gripped her shoulders. "Stop talking!"

Emma lunged for the knife on his belt. He spun her around, catching her in a choke hold. She jammed her elbow into his gut, and he whirled her around again, holding her inches from his sour face. His breath came in short bursts, and his nostrils flared.

Emma glared into his dark eyes. She hated him with a force that was twenty times her size, with a fury charred into her bones since her mother's death. She hated him for the father she'd never known, for every time Stan had gotten drunk and slapped her around. She hated him for the sadness that overwhelmed her mind and crushed her spirit.

"Do that again, and I'll kill you," he roared.

"Then do it!" she screamed right back at him.

Lines of disappointment creased his forehead. "Didn't know you were so tough," he said. "Expected you to be weak, like most women."

Emma's body tensed. He was right. Of all things she could be called, weak certainly wasn't one of them. Traumatized, yes. A rebel, maybe. Emotionally disturbed, definitely. But she was no wimp. Up until her mother's death, Emma had lived life on the edge. The first of her friends to bungee jump off a bridge, the first to drink herself into a stupor on a bet, earning her a month-long stint of community service and, later, rehab.

"My stupid Ma was weak." He snorted and spit on the ground. "Typical female. Until my father got sick of her cryin' all the time and beat her to a pulp. That toughened up her hide. She kept her big mouth shut, then. Maybe you oughta think about keeping your big mouth shut, too. Unless you wanna end up dead."

"Don't you threaten me!" Emma shouted. "I'm not afraid to die. In fact you'd be doing me a favor, so why don't you just shoot me or stab me or whatever and get it over with?"

He pressed his lips together until they were bloodless. Emma smirked. She'd won. He wasn't getting the reaction he wanted.

His eyes glazed over. "You shouldn't say things like that… it gives me ideas."

8

Tok lay on his side, his chest aching with each heaving breath. He would have scored a deep bite into Weasel Tail's hide, if only he hadn't been so weak from hunger. The few bites of food the girl had given him warmed his belly and his heart. He wasn't sure if he really liked the fond feelings he was developing for her. Best to stay neutral. Especially if she died—it would only make it that much harder for him. But, no matter how he tried, he couldn't help himself. Maybe it was the sadness in her eyes or the scars he'd seen on her pale body.

He rested his aching head on the cold ground, his tongue dry and swollen. Tok pressed his ears forward and lifted his muzzle to taste the air. He smelled the girl's scent growing stronger as she approached… when a hand touched his back, he stifled the urge to growl. Tok closed his eyes, such a gentle touch on his wretched hide. The girl parted bits of his bloodied fur to examine the oozing sores on his back. She touched a tender spot and he whined. The girl jerked her hand back, and then, cautiously, ran it over the rest of his protruding spine.

Her soft touch soothed his wild nature. He didn't want to like it. He couldn't weaken or he'd never survive. But he did like it and he let the warmth of her touch sink into his miserable body. So gentle. Never before had anyone, other than his mother, touched him with such a velvet caress. The girl's small hands paused at his sides where the sores from the buckles of the pack wore deep. She unsnapped the burdensome knapsack and rolled it aside. Tok inhaled a deep breath. For several months, he'd worn the pack without relief. He took another breath, letting his sore ribs expand fully, enjoying the freeing sensation while she inspected the rest of his wounds.

The girl sighed, reached into her pocket, and spread something thick and cool over his sores. What was it? It smelled oily, like whale blubber.

"There," she said, her voice soft as summer rain. "Nothing like good old petroleum jelly. Makes a cheap lipgloss. Never thought I'd be using it on a wolf."

She ran light fingers over his muzzle. "What do they call you? Hmmm? I think I should give you a name. How about 'Amarok?' It sounds cool and it means wolf." She stroked his fur. "What do you think of that?"

Tok wagged his tail, and she smiled. His wolf heart skipped. It was the first time he'd seen anything other than sadness cross her face. Tok felt a rush of joy. He'd made someone happy, someone who had helped him out of kindness. Maybe he hadn't lost that small part of himself that still belonged to mankind. And by making this girl smile, he had in some small way solved a part of his own unquenchable thirst for happiness.

His ruff bristled at the thought of his first cruel master, Abe Ryan, Weasel Tail's great-grandfather. Tok had loathed Abe with a deathless hatred. Abe's cruelty had known no bounds and Tok never forgot the stout rope the old man looped around his neck, cutting off his air. Nor would he forget how Abe's club had crushed his tender snout. Tok had vowed to never let another man put a rope around his neck and no one dared—not even Weasel Tail

Tok had learned to eat raw meat, no matter how loathsome. It turned his muscles hard as steel, and he'd grown callous to pain. As long as he had food his body remained invincible. But no matter what his condition, Tok was a skilled hunter. With his heightened senses, he could scent the wind and detect prey miles away. He could run with the swiftness of a deer and pull game down with the strength of a bear.

The morsels the girl had given him eased the clamor of his empty stomach, tiding him over until he could find something more substantial. Food would make him strong again, and then he could better protect her. Very soon he'd find something to kill. He only wished it could be Weasel Tail.

9

"Get up," Weasel Tail growled.

Emma's mouth fell open. "We can't go yet. He's hurt." She petted the sleeping wolf's head, remembering how her mother had brushed her hair when she was ill, untangling each knot so carefully. She'd do anything to feel those soothing brush strokes again.

"Get up now—or I'll make you get up!"

Emma ignored him and ran her fingers down the wolf's neck, loosening his bulky collar. She'd never get up; he'd have to kill her first. Out of the corner of her eye, she watched the man stalk off, his body tight and his fists clenched. He shrugged off his pack and reached inside. Was he getting a gun? Her heart ping-ponged. Hopefully he'd do it quickly. Then she'd be with her mother and she could tell her she was sorry. Tell her she loved her. Tell her she didn't mean all the hurtful things she had said.

The wolf raised his head and struggled to get up. Emma wrapped her hands around the bony ribcage and helped to pull the poor creature to his feet. The animal peered around her and whined as if in warning. Emma spun on her heel and faced her attacker, prepared for the worst. The man just stood there, staring at her with a mocking smile. He carried something, partially concealed in his hand, a Y-shaped stick with a large rubber band. A slingshot. He placed a stone in the center, pulled it back to his ear and aimed for her head.

She tried to duck, but the rock struck her shoulder. Pain, hot and searing, burned into her skin. Her chest heaved, and she gripped her arm. Tears stung her eyes.

"Get movin', or it'll be your eye next."

Emma hesitated, cradling her injured limb when another rock whizzed past her ear. She cut her eyes at him and clenched her jaw until her teeth ached.

He tapped the slingshot against the palm of his callused hand and narrowed his eyes.

"OKAY!" Emma snarled. "We're moving as fast as we can!"

"Well, it's not fast enough!" He scowled like a schoolyard bully, scanned the ground for a moment, and then picked up an even bigger rock. Snickering, he loaded the slingshot. Emma tried to bolt but the rock struck her knee.

She dropped to the ground, clutching her leg. He reloaded, pulled the weapon back again and let another rock fly. Emma froze as the stone zinged toward her face. The wolf jumped in front of her and took the blow to his ribs. The rock made a horrible thud as it ruptured the hide and stuck in his tender flank. The animal yelped and twisted in a tight circle, gnawing at his side. The man threw back his head and let loose a vicious laugh.

"Amarok!" Emma ignored the burning in her knee and knelt beside the wolf. Blood oozed from the wound where the rock protruded from the creature's flank. She steadied him, pulled out the stone, and threw the rock to the ground. Amarok dropped to his side and licked at the raw wound. Emma glared at her captor. He wore a satisfied grin.

Fury boiled in her blood. For a moment, Emma forgot how her exhausted body ached and her knee throbbed. She even forgot who she was—and what had happened to her mother—as a bitter, seething hatred ate at her brain. She charged her attacker and tackled him to the ground. Emma landed on top, pounding with her fists. She wanted to shatter his teeth, break his jaw, and split his lip so he'd never be able to flash that stupid smile again. He bucked his hips and flung her off of him, latched onto her arm, and dragged her to her feet. She kicked at him, jerked her arm away, and he shoved her hard ahead of him. The wolf came to her side, his muzzle lowered. She reached to touch his head when his ears suddenly pricked up. He lifted his nose, his mouth opened slightly. Sniffing the air, he jogged ahead a short ways, the scarlet wound oozing on his side. He paused, glanced back at her, and then broke into a lope over the rise.

"Amarok, come back!" Something about his leaving panicked her. He was wounded. She didn't want him to die. But more than that, she desperately needed him. He made her feel safe. He gave her a purpose.

"Keep your trap shut!" her captor said, packing away the slingshot. "Unless you feel like starving."

"What do you mean?"

"He's after our dinner."

Emma broke through the brush and up over a rise. She spotted Amarok a few yards ahead, working his way downhill into the valley. His body lowered almost to the ground, slowly stalking forward. Ahead of him, a shabby-looking caribou stood all alone. Amarok seemed reborn by the urge to kill. Her gaze strayed to the surrounding area. Caribou were herd animals, yet no other animals were nearby. This one must be either old or sick and close to death—an easy meal for a weak wolf.

The man snorted. "What did I tell you—dinner."

Emma shivered and turned away.

"You won't be so picky when I get you back to the cabin. You'll be too busy washing my clothes and chewing hides."

"Don't count on it!"

He frowned, his eyes burning into hers. He took a step closer and his gaze slipped up and down her body. "You know, you ain't all that pretty. At first I thought you was, with that long red hair and blue eyes, till I saw all them scars. Maybe you might be too marked up, even for a mountain man like me."

The jab hurt, even though she really didn't care what he thought. The mention of the scars brought more unwanted thoughts to the surface. She flinched and his eyes danced with enjoyment at her discomfort. He reached into his pocket and pulled out a pack of cigarettes, tapping the bottom a few times. His eyes shifted to the wolf. "He's deadly when his belly's full, and even more so when he's hungry." He selected a long white smoke, stuck it in his mouth, and lit the tip, polluting the air with the scent of cherry-menthol. The nauseating smell reminded her of Stan and his stinky cigars.

If only her mother had listened to her about him, none of this would have happened. Emma had fought hard to stay in Los Angeles, but her mother never wavered in her determination to relocate to be with Stan—a fiery prosecuting attorney for L.A. County. They'd moved to Alaska after Stan killed a man while driving drunk, and he'd needed a fresh start in his career. Stan might've hated losing the status of the job in California, but he'd never once shown an ounce of regret for ending someone's life. Stan had fooled her mother, but he couldn't fool her. Underneath that smooth veneer of a civilized servant of the people, Emma had sensed what he really was—a gutter rat—a dangerous, abusive man.

Emma's heart sank. She missed everything about Southern California: Venice Beach with its cozy cottages and scenic walkways, shopping down Melrose Avenue, hanging out at the arcade eating junk food with friends. She even missed the traffic on Hollywood Boulevard, and fighting the flood of tourists flocking to Disneyland on spring break. But most of all, she missed their cozy apartment on Fountain Avenue. She'd do anything to time-travel. To stick the key she still carried on her keychain into the sun-bleached door. To turn the doorknob, walk inside, and to smell her mother's famous chicken soup simmering on the stove.

Emma turned away, unable to watch as the wolf tore out the caribou's throat.

10

Tok liked the sound of his new name—Amarok. And he liked the way the girl whispered it when she caressed his rugged hide. The softness in her eyes when she spoke ignited a fire inside of him—a will to carry on living. A purpose to be alive, to be with her, to protect her. No longer would he be called Tok. Tok was a prisoner in a wolf's body—Amarok was the brave warrior inside the wolf. From now on he would be Amarok—just for her.

He remained at the kill, feasting on what Weasel Tail hadn't cut up and divided among their backpacks. With his belly filled, he returned from the valley to the hillside where Weasel Tail had built a fire and roasted a slab of meat. Even the girl ate, which made Amarok feel good. He liked providing for her as a man should. His soaring spirits crashed. Even with a new name, he still wasn't a man. He was a wolf, and she adored him like a pet dog. Still, he enjoyed her fond feelings.

For so long, his soul had been an empty void. Until now, he couldn't imagine how it was possible to feel anything but misery. This girl was his pinhole of light in an abyss of darkness. He curled protectively beside her, near the crackling fire, and chewed on a piece of antler he'd carried from the carcass. The calcium-rich snack would replace the minerals leached from his bones during weeks of utter starvation.

While he gnawed on the horn, he surveyed the area. He questioned Weasel Tail's judgment in setting up camp so close to the kill. The meat would draw predators from miles away. They were less than two days from the cabin, better to keep going. He hated to think of what Weasel Tail had in store for the girl, hated the thought of his filthy hands on her. If things got out of control, he'd rip the man's throat out. He would gladly sacrifice his own life for hers. He'd lived long enough, and what kind of a life did he have anyhow? One of abject misery and sorrow. Until the girl had come, he hadn't fully realized the cost of being a wolf, how he'd never be able to have a family of his own, or the comfort of a woman at his side.

Amarok watched the girl as she stared into the fire, her eyes filled with pain. More than being kidnapped troubled the girl, something far deeper. She didn't seem to care any more about her own life than he did for his. He wanted desperately to lean against her knee, and to feel her soothing touch, to reassure her that everything would be all right, even though he had his own doubts, but he had to stay alert and guard her.

Sleep tormented him like the scent of fresh blood. He longed to lay his muzzle on his paws and allow the food in his belly to lull him to sleep. With a little rest and the fuel in his gut, he'd be strong as steel again. His confidence escalated. No matter what happened, he'd be resilient enough to protect her now.

Weasel Tail rested near the fire, his head against his pack. At his feet, the girl curled up against a log, shivering in spite of the flames. While they slept, Amarok thought of all the tundra's hungry predators. He heard the calls of the pack of wolves that lived to the east, and the sneaky footsteps of an arctic fox. When he finally dozed off, his dreams were nightmarish. They kept him half-awake and he was glad. It enabled him to stay alert to any danger lurking nearby.

The yips and howls of the distant wolf pack increased in the hours just before daybreak. Without so much as snapping a twig or rustling a leaf, they crept like ghosts, peering from behind trees and snow-topped boulders. Amarok felt their piercing gaze, caught an occasional blur of movement, but none of this was of any real concern. What troubled him was the bloody carcass luring in the one beast that terrified him, the one creature who stalked the herds of mankind with an unyielding passion for revenge.

Suka.

Even the name sent adrenaline racing through his veins. He'd once been a wanted man—a bush-wise murderer who'd disappeared into the wilderness. Native legend said that in a drunken stupor Suka had stumbled too near the cursed valley, and the shaman had turned him into a monstrous bear. After his transformation, the old native had given the beast to the Ryan family, and in exchange they stalked the land, scouting for victims.

Suka had flown into a rage when Abe Ryan caged him, and only bars of steel could contain the furious beast. But even with ten-inch chains and iron bars, Abe Ryan couldn't control the bruin. One dark afternoon Suka broke his chains, killed Abe, and slashed the bear totem from the man's neck.

No longer a slave, and elated at finding his totem, Suka had waited for the transformation to begin, to live as a man once again. When it didn't happen he went mad, killing all that came near him or dared to enter his domain. For there was one thing Suka didn't understand, one thing Amarok had learned by listening to Abe explain to Weasel Tail. There were two totems carved of mammoth tusk for each transformed person—one hidden on the tainted soil of the cursed land, and one held by the Ryans. Both totems must be held to grant Suka—or any of the shaman's other victims—freedom. Even with possessing the first totem, finding the second one might prove impossible as it would mean venturing into Milak's forbidden land, risking disease and enslavement for anyone who tried.

Furious, Suka had retreated deep into the wilderness with his totem, not knowing about the second one that kept him in bear form. Wherever he traveled he slashed a symbol of four claws into the trees, marking his territory.

After a hundred years it was carved into the face of the earth across the vast wilderness, miles wide—a warning sign to those who entered his domain. For anyone who crossed Suka's path died.

Now, more than a century later, his rage and hatred increased with each passing year. There was no one Suka hated more than the Ryan family for the evil pact they held with Milak, a treaty formed long ago. Amarok had overheard stories, whispered by natives who traded goods with Weasel Tail, claiming that Abe Ryan was an animal transformed into human form to do Milak's bidding, and that all of Abe's descendants still carried some sort of animal trait.

Amarok had also heard others warn Weasel Tail of Suka's wrath, but he'd only laughed the stories off as tall tales. Young, stubborn, and dim-witted, he boasted of the day he'd kill the bear to avenge his great-grandfather. On more than one occasion he'd seen the bear lurking near the cabin, standing in the deadfall, shadow cast across the permafrost, waiting and watching for the right moment to attack. Amarok wanted more than anything for Suka to kill Weasel Tail, to watch the bear rip the cretin to pieces for all his cruelty. But now he dreaded a run-in with the great bear. Once Suka killed Weasel Tail, he'd be after the girl, and there would be little Amarok could do to protect her, even though he would die if need be to save her. He closed his eyes, trying to shut out the horrible images flashing through his mind.

The wind howled around him and through the trees. Amarok jumped to his feet. His wolf heart pounded. A groan settled across the terrain, speaking to him of the thousand ways in which the girl could die in this lawless land. No matter the cost, he'd stay strong to protect her.

Amarok shook the frost from his fur, turned eastward, and tipped his face to the welcome blush of daybreak.

11

Emma staggered behind her captor, sleep tugging at her eyelids. They'd risen at dawn to continue their trek to God only knew where. It didn't matter where they were headed. *Nothing* mattered anymore. She wanted out, and death held the door. Strange, how most people feared the end, and she welcomed it so openly. Emma wouldn't allow fear to control her, because there was one thing she had learned about it—fear didn't last long. It couldn't. It took too much energy to sustain. Just like all the times Stan burst into her room, violating her space in a drunken fury, mad about a dish left on the kitchen table or hair in the bathroom sink—any excuse to beat her, terrorize her.

The first few times he'd slapped her, she screamed until her throat was raw and her eyes red and swollen. But after those first blows, she'd gotten used to it, grown numb, and now he couldn't scare her anymore. She got power from silence. No matter what Stan did to her, he couldn't make her cry, couldn't make her beg, and he couldn't make her say she was sorry, not even when he beat her with his belt. Emma kept her focus on the muddy ground, occasionally glancing at Amarok to make sure he still walked by her side. At least he would be with her—at the end. She willed herself to think of nothing but the next step, and the next, until they arrived at whatever destination the creep had in mind.

They hiked through a mile of deadfall and into a shaded forest floor of clinging muck and slushy snow. The brisk morning air carried a heavy fragrance of wet pine and musky earth. Emma swallowed the dry lump in her throat. She'd kill for a caramel latte with whipped cream and sprinkles. She sighed, thinking of how many times she'd passed on getting one, obsessed with calories. Now she'd drink one after another, or anything else, for that matter. For the last mile, thirst had plagued her, leaving her throat scratchy and raw.

Emma tried to focus on her stride, but no matter how she struggled to forget, unwanted thoughts kept trickling in, the way hurtful memories did when she least expected or wanted them. Some small, stupid thing—a color, a smell, or even a word— would trigger a stampede of overwhelming thoughts.

She didn't want to know what might lie ahead. Death certainly didn't bother her. There were things much worse than dying, and she shuddered to think of them. She yearned to give up, to press her body against the earth, to dissolve into this untamed land that belonged to no one, to melt into the luminous void that stretched between earth and sky. But she couldn't lie down to rest, because this asshole had taken the only thing she'd had left—her freedom. First chance she got, she'd make him pay.

Emma stared daggers into the man's back. She could only imagine how terrible his cabin must be. If he touched her, forced her somehow, she'd find a way to kill him, then herself. She smiled. Maybe she'd blow the place up and make a big, grand exit. Her heart fell and she paused, staring at her companion. If something happened to her, then what would happen to Amarok? He trotted to her side, faithful as ever, staring up at her with those liquid pools of undying sorrow.

"Sure wish you could speak," she said. "Or understand what I'm telling you. Maybe you wouldn't like me so much if you knew that I killed my own mother. Would you still like me then, Amarok?"

He wagged his tail as if in answer and she patted his broad head.

"It's all my fault," she whispered, her throat hoarse. She knelt down in front of him, and the dam broke. Hot tears streamed down her face. "I went into my bedroom that night and I waited until everyone was asleep." Amarok tilted his head and rested on his haunches, his eyes finding hers. Emma shook her head. Why was she telling him all this? Maybe it was knowing she was nearing the end of her life, and she no longer wished to carry the burden to her grave. "I snuck out my bedroom window and hitched a ride into town with friends. We got wasted drunk. Mom woke up at midnight, found out I was missing, and went looking for me. The roads were sheets of ice. Emergency travel only." More tears flowed. "She ran off the highway and plunged into the river… and drowned. All because of me. If only I'd stayed home that night, she wouldn't be dead. She'd still be alive—if it weren't for me."

Amarok licked her face, making Emma jump. She smiled sadly and wiped the saliva off with the back of her hand. "So, you do still like me. Don't you?" She hugged his neck. "At least I still have you."

The man stopped a few yards ahead. "Get moving!"

Emma stood, wiped the tears blurring her vision, and forced herself onward. Amarok stayed nearby, nipping at her hands and nudging her playfully when she grew tired. Up ahead, Emma heard the hypnotic rush of water. She licked her dry lips and swallowed hard as she hurried down the narrow trail. Amarok squeezed past her, loping ahead. Emma jogged after him, ducking under a series of low-hanging branches. They came to a rocky area where a rushing waterfall flowed into a mossy stream. For a moment Emma stood still, lulled by the roar of the water's liquid blade cutting down the glacial mountainside. She leaned against the rocks and guzzled from the cool, clear brook, swallowing the refreshing liquid until her belly hurt. Emma doubted she'd ever tasted anything so cold and pure.

The man filled a large canteen and stuffed it into his pack. As Amarok drank from one of the smaller pools, Emma noticed something golden reflecting in the translucent water. She knelt near Amarok for a closer look and spotted a flash of red. A school of tiny fish drifted peacefully, occasionally flashing bits of white when they opened their mouths to feed on bits of moss. Hypnotized by the soothing sound of the flowing water and tranquil dance of minnows, she almost forgot how much she had grown to hate water. After her mother's death, she hated all rivers, all lakes and streams. They stood as symbols of something taken from her. But now, gazing at the small fish, with the refreshing liquid energizing her body, she saw that water could also give life.

"Don't just sit there gawking all day! Get a move on!" the man barked, interrupting the serene moment.

Emma turned to leave when she spotted something near Amarok's paw. "Oh, my God!"

The man jerked to a stop. "What?"

Emma pointed to a huge footprint in the mud. "What kind of a track is that?"

The man peered at the print and grumbled underneath his breath. "Bear track. A big one." He sneered at Emma. "Better keep up or it might get ya."

Emma gawked at the track, eyes wide with fright. The indents from the giant claws were at least six inches long.

A vein throbbed in the man's forehead and he ground his teeth together. He mashed the track into the mud with the tip of his boot, and then turned and stomped down the trail. "Get a move on!" he barked.

He seemed more agitated than usual, pressing them on at a faster pace. Emma's nerves knotted at the thought of a bear attack. What had they taught her at school? Drop and play dead? Run downhill? A wave of fear coursed through her. She couldn't remember! She glanced at Amarok, who'd seemed filled with vigor since his recent meal. He gazed at her and his large yellow eyes filled with affection. Emma's nerves settled. Amarok would never let anything hurt her. She wasn't sure how or why she felt this way. He was, after all, just a wolf, but he seemed to want to protect her. Even when she was sad, he somehow sensed it.

They continued northward down the flank of the mountain. Amarok trotted at Emma's side, veering off every so often into the trees, only to return moments later. Every time he strayed it filled Emma with unease. An unfamiliar wave of vulnerability washed over her. She was strong, she was smart, and she had more guts than most people. Even so, Emma knew she couldn't survive without the wolf's protection.

12

By nightfall they crossed into a wide valley at the edge of the sea. Ice floes glittered in the pale moonlight, winking as if heaped with diamonds. Amarok paused, surveying the valley, uneasy to be in the open expanse. He much preferred the safety of the mountains, the shelter of trees. He knew the trail would lead them back to the safety of the timber, but he remained vigilant.

The girl stumbled several times on the trail and Amarok's heart filled with concern. He knew she must be exhausted. She'd been through so much, yet she proved to have an iron will. A fighter. He admired her courage. Yet her fearlessness with death concerned him, as if she longed for it as a way to escape her sorrow. If only he could make her see she had so much to live for, but how could he ever do that?

Amarok stood still and sniffed the wind, letting the girl and man pass by him. A dark shadow sailed overhead. Amarok spotted an owl sailing across the milky sky, circling over his head before disappearing into the night. Something about it caused him to pause as he watched it disappear, leaving a single, silver feather spiraling to the ground. The object landed at his front paw and Amarok studied it carefully. He gently gathered the feather between his teeth and tucked it into a strap at his shoulder.

Hours later, they made camp at the base of Wolverine Range, with the night so cold Amarok feared the girl might freeze to death before Weasel Tail managed to build an adequate fire. She'd need to rest for the next day's journey. He knew she must be hungry, if not starving, by this time. She fell asleep quickly, wrapped in a scrap of caribou hide Weasel Tail kept in his pack. Amarok watched over her as she slept, tucking himself around her for warmth, keeping guard until sleep pulled his eyes closed.

He thought about what the girl had told him, how much pain she carried over the death of her mother. He knew what it was like to lose someone he loved more than life. It seemed all he'd ever done was lose. First his father and mother and then his human life. It seemed so unfair. And yet he lived on and on by the same evil that had murdered everyone he loved. Even in wolf form, he was glad to be alive, his lifespan reaching far enough to have met this beautiful girl, to have experienced her gentle touch on his wretched hide.

Perhaps to feel love again.

13

Emma woke the next morning so cold and stiff she could hardly move. Weasel Tail had boiled water over the fire and made something that smelled like coffee, although she'd never drink any of it, not that he'd offered. Something brushed against her hand and she frowned. A single white feather caressed her skin. Emma picked it up. Where had it come from? Resting a few feet away, Emma saw Amarok watching her. There was a soft expression in his eyes—a mischievous glow. Could the wolf have given her the feather as a gift? She picked it up and twirled it by the stem. The wolf's ears perked playfully. Emma smiled. So, maybe it had been the wolf, after all.

The man kicked dirt and snow over the fire and emptied his cup into the waning embers. Steam hissed into the air and Emma got to her feet, blowing warm air over her hands. She stepped back as the man rolled up the hides and shoved them into his pack. She wondered when it would ever end. She didn't know how much longer she could handle the cold and the endless journey.

The wolf jogged to her and sat at her feet. Emma tucked the feather behind her ear, rubbed Amarok's head, and surveyed the area. They'd camped at the base of a mountain range not far from the sea. Even if she managed to escape now, she'd have no idea which way was home, unless the wolf helped her, but he seemed to be under total control of the creep. Why didn't he fight back more? Why did he return after hunting instead of just running away?

Emma wondered if the wolf missed his pack as much as she missed her mother. Maybe he'd never known his wolf pack. At least she'd gotten to have a mother until she was seventeen, almost grown. But it wasn't long enough. She wanted more time and that just wasn't possible.

14

They crunched along the frosty trail leading to the Wolverine Mountains. Prospectors had cursed this long trek to the remote mountain range as a backbreaker, full of devil's-claw, icy fords, deadfalls, and avalanches. Amarok worried about the girl and how lightly dressed she was, even though it was still early fall. Amarok's mind stretched back to a time when the mercury in the thermometer outside old man Ryan's door had frozen solid at nearly forty-degrees below zero in late October. Now, the weather patterns were less extreme but still unpredictable. It could turn for the worse at any time, and the girl would be unprepared—perhaps even die from exposure. Fear crawled over him. He could barely protect himself, let alone another creature, in the remote Alaskan wilds.

Wildlife tracks, rimmed with ice, littered the trail. Frost glistened along the bases of spruce trees and fallen birch leaves shivered under the steady beat of polar winds. Heavy rain clouds seethed overhead and soon unloaded their heavy burdens in a violent, chilly downpour. They took shelter under a natural lean-to made of brush and deadfall, waiting out the storm. Amarok was glad for the break—the girl needed it. She'd grown paler and wearier the longer she'd staggered up the trail. Still, she'd used what energy she'd had to run her fingers along his back, to stroke his head, or to see where he'd gone when he veered off the path. He'd never strayed very far, knowing the girl needed him. He much preferred her company to scouting the landscape.

After the rain stopped, they traveled for hours until exhaustion forced them to stop for the night. They set up camp in a tree line, near the frigid banks of an oxbow lake. The wind rushed over the small encampment, threatening to stifle the waning flames of the campfire. Amarok curled up next to the girl, and she wrapped her arm around his weary hide. She lay so still beside him, her breath feathering his ruff, appearing to sleep the deep, dreamless slumber of total exhaustion. Amarok, however, didn't sleep. His gaze continuously swept across the storm-blasted expanse. What his eyes couldn't see, his other senses would tell him. He tasted the wind and, although it gave him no clue, he knew Suka lurked somewhere in the darkness. Hungry. Hunting. Hating.

Amarok longed to rise and scout the outskirts of the camp, but the girl needed his warmth. When he'd tried, she'd stirred and clasped onto him tighter. He didn't want to disturb her sleep. She'd need all the energy she had in order to survive. Amarok spied Weasel Tail, also awake, with his arm around his rifle. He'd moved to the other side of the fire. Amarok had sensed the man's fear from the moment he spotted Suka's track in the shallow pool. If the bear attacked, Amarok would keep his focus on protecting the girl and let the man fend for himself.

He thought of the misery the girl endured. She was like a sparrow with broken wings, kicked out of the comfort of the nest. He understood the razor-sharp pain that cut into her soul, the guilt and utter despair. How could she believe she was to blame? The girl was a kind-hearted person with a nurturing soul. If only he could tell her she wasn't the cause of any of it. Amarok laid his head on his paws, overcome with emotions as rugged and raw as the glacier-ridden mountains before him.

At dawn Amarok got to his feet, careful not to disturb the girl, and worked his way to a high perch on a steep hillside. He peered down upon the earth, into the ice-choked canyons and across to the barren tundra valley. So many winters had passed before his eyes, and as the seasons changed, his life remained much the same. Throughout his long servitude, he'd missed the companionship of another human being. Cruel Abe Ryan could hardly be called a companion and his grandson, Weasel Tail, was a man to be hated. But Suka, with his bloodlust, was a breed of crazy that Amarok feared more than anything else.

When Amarok was young, he never knew such people existed; he'd only read stories of villains in Wild West tales. His legs trembled as he remembered the dreadful look in his father's eyes when they'd crossed paths with Suka on the way to check their trap lines. Suka stood at the edge of the trail, partially concealed in the bushes, his flannel shirt stained with sweat and blood. He clutched a doll in one hand and a knife in the other. Coins glistened in sun, protruding from a jagged slash in the doll's back.

The wild, piercing look in Suka's eyes made Amarok's neck stiffen. Suka held the knife in front of him, waving it at them as they passed at a healthy distance. Later, word came that Suka had murdered a woman and her four children for gold—slashing their throats. No wonder his shirt had been soaked in blood.

Amarok closed his eyes, blocking out the haunting image.

A voice sang out his name, carried softly on an arctic breeze. Amarok stood still and listened, hearing the girl's call. He wheeled and ran to the campsite. She greeted him with a smile, patting her leg, beckoning him to her side. Amarok loped to her, sinking to his haunches as she hugged his neck.

15

Emma's kidnapper had jumped when she yelled for the wolf. He seemed more anxious than ever before, narrowing his eyes, glaring at her as she stroked Amarok's fur. The man stood completely still. His gaze slid away, darting over the landscape, endlessly scanning. Minutes slipped past, and Emma wondered if he'd ever move again. A few minutes later, he turned his back and stomped into the brush. Emma thought about making a break for it, but he quickly returned, zipping up his pants. He shoved the caribou hides they'd slept on into his pack and kicked snow over what remained of the fire.

Overhead, an owl soared across the early morning sky, its white winter plumage a pale discoloration against the gloomy clouds. It swooped low, sailing several times over Amarok's head as if following him, watching him, and then disappeared into the gray horizon. Emma ran her fingers over the silky feather, safely tucking it behind her ear.

They traveled in the same direction as the bird, heading north at a hard pace. Rain drizzled from the sky again, which made the trek even worse. Wet and cold were a harsh mix in the arctic. Emma could never get warm enough with the polar winds and the constant dampness. Her hair stuck to her skull like a helmet. She would've given anything for a hot shower. She hated smelling like smoke, hated the grime on her face and hands, but most of all, she hated smelling like *him*—the man who'd taken away her last shimmer of hope. No matter what, she would make him pay. She'd make things hard for him; she'd never be a willing participant in his sick plan. Mule-stubborn, she'd dig her heels in, like she'd done with Stan. And just like Stan, this man would never make her do what he wanted. He could never break her will—she'd gladly die first.

The rain disappeared around noon, when they entered an area clogged with deadfall and thick clumps of underbrush. Emma crossed a fallen log, and a sheer pain jabbed into her foot. "Ouch!" She hopped on one leg. "Can we stop for a second? There's something wrong with my heel."

The man stopped, swiveled around slowly and narrowed his eyes to slits. "You got two minutes. Better make it quick." He leaned against a boulder, arms folded, leering at her.

Emma balanced against the trunk of a spruce tree, slipped off her boot, pulled her sock down, and winced. Angry blisters, red and raw, swelled across her ankle. She eased the sock back over her blisters when she noticed a tree branch wave in the distance, then another. Something was headed their way. Something big. Amarok laid back his ears and growled, baring his teeth. His body stiffened, and his tail hung parallel to the ground. A deer bounded from the trees and skittered away.

Emma breathed a sigh of relief and slipped her boot on, but Amarok still growled, his fur bristling higher. She patted his broad head. "It's okay, boy, it was just a deer."

Amarok stalked forward, snarling louder, ignoring her touch. *What was wrong with him?*

A sudden, violent thrashing from the brush brought Weasel Tail to his feet. He pulled a long rifle from the side of his pack.

Emma stepped back, staring into the brush, every nerve in her body on fire.

"What was that?"

"Hush!" the man hissed. He shouldered the rifle and peered through the sights into the timber.

Minutes passed. She held her breath. A booming crash sounded. Then another, closer this time. He shoved her to the ground and onto her belly. "Stay there!" The man crept ahead, surveying the area. With her nose close to the ground, Emma's nostrils filled with the musty smell of wet leaves and rotting plants, wilted with frost. The man turned and waved her up. Emma rose from the ground, her damp clothes clinging to the front of her body, sending a deep chill into her bones.

He placed a finger to his lips and pulled her to him. He pressed his mouth to her ear. "Listen," he whispered. "A grizzly's favorite trick is to roar, then circle around back while the prey's lookin' ahead." His eyes drifted over the terrain and then to Amarok. "The wolf will let us know where the bear's at."

Terror washed over Emma in a freezing wave, and she glanced at Amarok. He stood protectively in front of her, ears erect, his gaze fixed into the brush behind her. His lips drew back, and a rumbling growl emanated from his throat. The man swung around and raised the rifle to his shoulder. A massive grizzly tore through the brush, galloping at them, its head held close to the ground, its mouth hanging open. Bands of foaming saliva flew out behind it.

Emma stood frozen. Unflinching, her captor fired a quick shot and missed. The deafening boom echoed through the woods. Emma covered her ears to stop the painful ringing searing into her eardrums. The bear kept coming and the man fired again. This time, the bullet sank deep into the creature's shoulder. The grizzly stumbled, almost collapsed, and continued its charge, even more enraged. The man fired another booming shot; a wad of flesh flew off the bear's mammoth hump with a splash of dark liquid. The beast lurched to a halt, wheeled and retreated into the forest.

Over the ringing in her ears, Emma heard the sounds of the grizzly disappearing deeper into the thick underbrush. Shaken, she dropped to her knees in the snow, trembling as she fought to gain control over the sudden rush of terror. Relief turned her bones into jelly, making it hard to stand.

Her captor spat on the ground. "Get up."

"Where are we going?"

"You'll see." He lowered the rifle at her. "Now, get up before I make you get up."

Emma rose to her feet, her nerves blazing. She tramped through the snow behind him. Her pulse quickened at every sound. The grizzly could return at any moment, tearing them to pieces and eating their flesh. She brought her shaking hands to her face, wiping the cold sweat from her forehead. Her legs wobbled as she scanned the forest, searching for danger. She felt herself starting to disconnect, floating from her body. Emma leaned against the base of a spruce tree. A flock of ravens flew from its branches, flapping over her head. She screamed, and the man grabbed her arm, his eyes wide with fright.

"What is it?" he roared.

She stood staring at him, fighting to catch her breath.

He dropped her arm and aimed the rifle at her head. "Make me jump like that again, and I'll put a bullet in your brain."

"I-I'm sorry," Emma stammered.

With a grunt, he lowered the gun. "We're almost there. Keep your trap shut."

Amarok came to her side, licking her hand. She ran her fingers over his bristly fur. The wolf trotted away, scouting the tree line, sniffing and pacing nervously. The man whistled and Amarok returned.

They trudged onward. Emma struggled through snow and mud that sucked at her oversized boots, crossing tangles of fallen trees stacked like matchsticks. Branches tore at her clothes and cut into her exposed skin until she collapsed from near exhaustion. Amarok rushed to her, licking her face. He wagged his tail and gave her a playful bark. She gazed into his sparkling eyes. Why was he suddenly so happy? Then it came to her, and her spirits soared. Maybe they were almost there, and the whole nightmare would be over soon.

Emma got to her feet, and after a short while they emerged into a clearing. A rustic log cabin with a mossy roof sat nestled in the middle, surrounded by several crude outbuildings. Traps hung from the eaves of the cabin, swaying with each gust of bitter wind.

Finally, she could stop hiking and get rid of the bulky boots. She fell to her knees, limbs quivering. Amarok jogged to her side, nudging her, as usual. A twig snapped. Her head jerked up. Amarok growled, and Emma saw the bleeding bear crash through the brush, surging straight at her.

"Look out!" the man roared.

She couldn't move. Her legs were like Jell-O. She fought to get to her feet, staring at the snarling mouth, the gigantic teeth of the furious beast raging closer and closer. It was at this moment that Emma suddenly realized how much she wanted to live.

"Run!" the man yelled.

Emma looked away as the bear slid to a stop at her feet, suddenly changing direction. It whirled and tackled the man before he could fire a shot, sinking its teeth into his thigh. The man screamed—an unearthly cry—pulled his knife from its sheath, and gouged at the bear. The grizzly knocked the blade from his hand and gripped the man's head in its powerful jaws, violently shaking him.

Emma bolted, glancing over her shoulder, running clumsily in the oversized boots. The bear dropped the man to charge after her. She ran for the cabin and tripped, her boots stuck in the snow. The bear barreled down on her. Amarok jumped between them, the two animal bodies blending into a growling mass of blood and fur. Emma scrambled to her feet, running hard to the cabin door. She gripped the handle. *Please don't be locked. Please!* She pushed the door open—*Thank God!*—and burst inside. She crouched under a dingy window, watching helplessly as the bear destroyed her only friend.

16

Just as Amarok had feared, Suka dropped Weasel Tail, broken and useless, to the ground, and headed straight for the girl. *His* girl. Amarok's hackles bristled as he raced to intercept the ungodly creature. His heart filled with fear and a sorrow so penetrating, he nearly lost himself in the enormity of the emotions. The end had finally come. Amarok prayed the girl would make it to the safety of the cabin before the bear butchered him.

Suka rose on his back legs, a deadly mountain of teeth and claws. With one powerful blow, he knocked Amarok back several feet. His vision blurred and his ears rang as his head throbbed from the painful blow. He scrabbled to his paws and leapt at the bear again. He couldn't let him get to the girl.

Amarok sank his teeth into Suka's neck. The great bruin flung him off again and charged after the girl. Amarok got in front of him, but Suka swiped his side, splitting it open with his claws. Intense heat burned like a brand, searing into his flesh.

Amarok hesitated, disabled by the pain. Suka seized the moment, unleashing the depth of his fury.

Every blow threw Amarok harder and harder to the ground. He tried to bite at the bear's tender spots, but Suka grabbed him by the shoulder in crushing jaws, biting down until Amarok howled, a thunderous scream of death.

The world swirled around him in a dazed mix of pain and regret. White lights flickered in front of his eyes, and for a brief moment he saw his mother dancing with the northern lights, her glossy hair decorated in beads and feathers. She reached out to him, beckoning him to the spirit world. He ached to let go, to find the peace he had so often dreamed of, but suddenly his mother wore the girl's face, and he wanted more than anything to stay.

The gentle images faded, and he slipped back into the brutal reality of agonizing death.

17

Emma clenched her jaw. *No! She wouldn't let this happen!* She whipped her head around, searching the cabin for a weapon. A club, a knife… anything! Finally, she spotted the stock of a gun sticking out from under a saggy twin bed. She ran, dropped to her knees and pulled it out. She clutched the beat-up rifle, flung the door open, fired, and missed.

The kick of the gun smashed into her shoulder, and with a yelp Emma flew backward onto the floorboards. The rifle spun away from her hands and rattled across the floor. Emma scrambled for the firearm, set it against her shoulder, and winced. She knew it would bruise, but she didn't care. She pulled the trigger again and shut her eyes, but nothing happened. She screamed in anger and pulled the trigger again. The grizzly heard her cry, lifted its giant head, and sniffed. With a roar, the bear left Amarok in a bloody heap and charged. Emma rushed to bar the door, but then spotted a lever sticking out the side of the gun. An image of her stepfather, Stan, flashed into her mind. *What did he do when he shot at gophers?* It suddenly came to her. She slapped up the lever and it knocked the bolt loose. Emma pulled it back and slammed it forward. With a click it locked down, and she pointed it back at the beast. The ground shook beneath her as the massive grizzly neared. She squeezed the trigger again, and this time it fired. The sound cracked across the space between them and landed somewhere in the bear's neck. The grizzly slid to a stop, shook its head, and staggered away into the brush.

Emma kept the gun raised and crept to Amarok. A rustling came from the brush behind her. She whirled around, her heart battering against her ribcage. She stared into the woods, searching. Tree limbs shook. Emma held her breath, fighting the urge to disconnect, to escape the suffocating terror. She focused on Amarok while she inched forward, keeping the gun raised. Her throat went dry, her breath suspended. How many bullets did she have left? Emma glanced at the cabin, and then to the spot where the grizzly had retreated. If it returned, she'd never make it to safety in time.

She reached down, snatched Amarok's collar and pulled him toward the cabin, all the while on the lookout for the bear. She strained under the dead weight and cringed, thinking how it must pain him to be dragged across the ground while so badly wounded. Sweat poured down her face by the time she reached the cabin. She hauled Amarok inside, bolted the door, and dragged him next to the cold hearth. His chest rose and fell, but his eyes remained cold and fixed.

Emma's tears fell onto his blood-soaked fur, and he shivered beneath her touch. "Please, Amarok. Please don't die. I need you." Sadness strangled her throat. "I'll get you warm, then I'll fix those wounds. Everything will be okay. It has to."

She rushed to the fireplace, grabbed a handful of dried twigs from the metal box next to the hearth, and tossed a log on top. Emma ran her fingers over the mantle and found a book of matches. Her hands shook as she struck a match against the strip on the side of the booklet. She held it to the twigs and watched the yellow flame catch and dance over the dry wood. The small fire simmered into a roaring blaze. Emma scanned the filthy interior, doubting she'd find anything resembling disinfectant to clean Amarok's wounds. The whole cabin stood in disarray. Rough-cut timber made up the floor; two chairs carved from logs sat near the hearth. A table covered in hides, a ratty twin bed, and an old army chest were crammed into a corner.

A small kitchen contained a rusty woodstove, basin, and hand pump. Emma rushed to the sink, pumped water into a bucket, and grabbed a dirty hand towel. She rinsed the cloth until the water ran clear, and knelt at Amarok's side.

Deep gashes and puncture wounds from Suka's teeth covered his side. Blood. So much blood. She wiped away the dirt and grime, and with it came chunks of flesh and fur. The more she wiped, the more hair he lost from his ragged coat.

She could tend to the deepest of cuts on her own body, but it broke her heart to see them riddled across Amarok's brittle frame. Why did this have to happen? She gritted her teeth and narrowed her eyes at the ceiling. Why did she have to suffer one more loss in her life? Emma hated death, the finality of it all—no second chances. The helplessness. She barely clung to the ledge of sanity and if Amarok died, she'd let herself fall, spiral away into an endless sleep.

Emma returned to the sink, rinsing out the bloody rags. She eyed a large butcher knife resting near the sink and longed to run the blade across her skin, to release the utter panic filling her head, burning through her body. A physical wound was something she could treat, tend to, and control. But no matter how she tried, she couldn't fix the pain and worry welling up inside, an unreachable suffering. Emma picked up the knife. The blade glinted in the shadowy light. Such a nice, sharp edge—it would make a long, thin cut. She gently slipped the dull side across her wrist and closed her eyes, savoring the feel of the cool, crisp steel against her fevered skin. Her eyes snapped open and she tossed the knife onto the kitchen table. What was she thinking? Cutting only brought more despair.

18

Amarok lay in a daze, his body riddled with misery so great he could hardly breathe. Although weak from loss of blood, his heart still pumped with triumph. He had done it. He had saved the girl, and somehow she'd managed to save him as well, even though it wouldn't be for long. Every bone ached, many seemed broken, and as his brain swelled, his vision blurred even more.

His spine went rigid as thoughts of Suka tormented him. The bear would be back, and then who would protect the girl? He knew she would never find the cache where Weasel Tail hid his supplies and ammunition. Without food or a way to protect herself, how would she ever make it out alive? The troublesome thoughts heightened the agony coursing through his ruined body. At least she was alive, for now, and he was grateful.

Amarok forced himself to relax, letting the pain envelop him, praying death would be swift, relieve him of the terrible burden.

He also prayed for the girl's safety, for the Great Spirit to protect her on her journey down the mountain to freedom.

The girl's soft hands touched his battered body, and his raw nerves fired like lightning growling from the sky. She ran her hand over his nose and he licked her fingers. The girl began to cry, and her whimpering hurt his heart as much as the wounds searing across his flesh hurt his body.

Death, he whispered silently, *please come swiftly.*

19

Emma cleaned the rest of Amarok's wounds and searched for something to bandage them with. She knew it would do little good—his injuries were too great—but she refused to give in, to let him slip away. She watched his chest heave, his breathing rapid. Her gut twisted at the sacrifice he'd made for her. In one selfless act, this kind and beautiful creature had given his own life to save hers, and suddenly she felt ashamed. Shame for all the times she'd so carelessly stalked death, walking close to the edge. Amarok had done nothing when the bear attacked the man, but when it had turned on her, he hadn't even hesitated. More tears came, which surprised her. She didn't think she had any moisture left.

Emma got to her feet and searched the grimy kitchen. She eyed the chest near the foot of the rumpled bed. Racing to it, she flipped open the lid to find a dusty stack of sheets. She started to pull them out, but felt hard, square objects wrapped inside.

She unwrapped them to find black and white pictures in glass frames. She set them aside and hurried to Amarok. She didn't have time to look at them now. Emma shook the dust from the linens, tore them into strips, and knelt to wrap his wounds.

She carefully bound the cloth around his bloodied body. So many injuries covered his wounded frame, she might as well cover him in one giant sheet. When she was done, she noticed his breathing seemed shallower.

"No, please, Amarok," Emma whispered. "Live for me, as selfish as it sounds." She sobbed. "I need you."

She ran her hand over his broad head. She would give anything to feel him gently nudge her, or give her a playful nip as he had done so many times on the trail, pressing her onward, giving her hope—a reason for her to exist in the darkness.

Cold emptiness filled Emma's heart. Her eyes strayed to the knife on the kitchen table. The sharp edge glinted seductively. She looked away, fighting the addiction to cut as the pain of withdrawal stabbed at her insides.

Emma shivered and glanced at the fireplace. Her heart lifted. The flames had gone out and with that came a task, something she could do to make things better. She would keep the fire stoked and the heat would heal Amarok. Everything would be okay and together they'd walk down the mountain. She'd even take him to California with her. Somewhere in the back of her mind, she knew it wasn't true, that he probably wouldn't make it, but she wouldn't allow the terrible thought to fully surface. Emma added more wood and stoked the fire into an energetic blaze.

Amarok lay very still. She grabbed a blanket from the bed and draped it over him. Emma examined the rest of the room and shuddered. She couldn't imagine living in such a dump. Who was this guy? And why had he kidnapped her? Was it just some random act of a madman? She returned to the trunk; crudely carved into the lid was a name, "Ryan." A first or last name? Emma sorted through the photographs, searching for answers. A wolf—one with identical markings to Amarok—was in many of them. Beside the wolf stood a man holding up some kind of ivory carving on a long leather cord. The man gleamed in the pictures, while the wolf cowered.

She took the photos to the window for better light. Sure enough, the wolf featured had white tips on the ends of its tail and forelegs and wore an identical collar. Maybe it was one of Amarok's ancestors. In the background, perched in a stand of trees, was the blurry outline of a great bird—an owl.

A bloody hand bashed against the window. Emma screamed and dropped the pictures to the floor. The hand banged on the glass again. She peered through the window and saw her captor, lying under the windowsill in a pool of blood. *Why wasn't he dead?*

"Help me," he growled through the glass.

"No!"

He kept banging until the panes shook. The man pulled himself up until his mangled face pressed against the window, his eyes fixed on Amarok. He held up an ivory object on a leather cord, leered at Emma with blood-encrusted teeth and squeezed it. Amarok let out a strangled cry, kicking his legs as if trying to escape some kind of suffocating pain. The man released the object and all was quiet again.

"Help me or I'll kill him."

"Never!" Emma roared.

The man squeezed the object again, blood dripping from the corner of his mouth. Amarok let out another weak cry and his chest heaved.

"What are you doing to him?"

"Get me inside or I'll kill him," the man gasped.

Emma hesitated and he wrapped his fingers around the object again.

"NO! Don't!"

Her mind raced. How could an object have so much control over Amarok? Could it be some kind of shock collar? Whatever it was—she had to get the object away from him. Emma went to the door, gun in hand. She could just shoot him and then take the object. Her chest constricted, and then suddenly deflated. Who was she kidding? She couldn't intentionally kill someone. Her mind drifted to her mother with that sudden realization. Yes, it was true. She had snuck out the night of her mother's accident, but she hadn't meant for her mother to die. She was no killer.

She hesitated at the door and glanced at the wolf. A chilling thought raced into her brain. Maybe she would have to kill— if it meant saving Amarok. Emma unlocked the door, and the wounded man shoved it open, grabbing her leg.

20

A loud bang broke through the haze in Amarok's head. He'd heard his master's voice ordering the girl to let him in, and felt the air rush from his lungs as Weasel Tail squeezed the totem. Spots of lights danced in front of eyes; pain shot into his jaw. His heart sank. Even in the clutches of death he couldn't escape the yoke of slavery. Then the pressure released and his lungs expanded. Maybe Weasel Tail had finally died. He could only hope. His head grew fuzzy as his body convulsed in shock.

Drums beat somewhere in the distance and he felt his spirit rising. In a mist, he saw a vision of his native ancestors hunting caribou and elk. A light filled with love glowed in the sky above him. Amarok tipped his nose to the radiant beam and sang. He sang for all the years he'd lost, and he sang of imprisonment, and of sorrow. Most of all he sang for the girl, for her life to be blessed and filled with his love, to carry with her for all time.

The ancient warriors drifted into nothingness as the light faded and the pain returned—horrible pain stronger than Suka's blows. Amarok felt his spirit fall, jolting back into his body. He opened his eyes and rubbed his aching head. Hands? He had hands? He closed his eyes and opened them again. He examined the back of his hand as if it were a rare jewel. A century had passed since he'd seen his true form. Amarok stared down at his human flesh in wonder. Pain seized his chest. He struggled to take another breath. At least in death, the girl would see that he was really a man and not just a wolf. If she hurried, maybe he could manage to find the strength to say goodbye, and the courage to tell her he loved her.

21

Emma kicked loose from the man's grasp and fell hard to her knees. He growled, inches from her face, his breath heavy with the rusty scent of blood. She scuttled backward and got to her feet just as he reached for her again, snatching her pant leg. She jerked away, struck him with the butt of the gun and he rolled, lifeless, onto his back. His eyes fixed in a death stare, gawking up at the sky. Emma glared at him, worn out, drained, not an ounce of emotion left—except anger. She ripped the totem from his hand and hurried inside.

Shoving the door closed, she leaned her shoulder into it to force his body out of the way and flipped the deadbolt. Emma sagged against the doorframe and examined the intricately carved item in her hand. It appeared to be ivory, yellowed with age, in the shape of a wolf. She glanced at Amarok. Her mouth flew open, the object falling from her grasp, forgotten.

A teenage boy lay curled under the blanket near the fire, his back to her and his lean body riddled with cuts and scrapes. His long, black hair fanned across the floor behind him.

What had he done with Amarok? Emma held the rifle in front of her and crept closer. "Who are you?"

The boy didn't answer. Whoever he was, he was badly injured. He lay unresponsive and she knelt next to him, but not too close, in case it was a trick. His wounds—his wounds were the exact same injuries Amarok had suffered. Looking at the bandages, she recognized her own handiwork. What was going on? None of this made any sense.

"Who are you?" Emma whispered.

He turned his head slowly, as if even slight movement pained him, and peered at her with heavy-lidded eyes. "Amarok."

Emma blinked in stunned silence and the boy inhaled a raspy breath.

"What did you say?"

"I am Amarok. The name you gave me…"

The boy's eyes closed and he lay very still. Her mind raced. How could he know the name she'd given the wolf? Could it be a coincidence? Or was it really Amarok? Emma shook her head. No, it wasn't possible. The world swam around her. She was tired. She was hungry. She needed a shower. Shit, she was losing her mind. Her throat locked up. Emma struggled for air, closing her eyes to calm her frayed nerves. Finally, her muscles relaxed, and she inhaled one soothing breath after another. She stumbled to a chair, and sat down heavily as she spied a discarded wolf pelt lying next to the boy. There was no question. Somehow this teenager was the wolf she had grown to care so much about, and now he lay in the throes of death. If magic had created him, then somehow, maybe magic could save him.

She got onto her knees and cradled his head in her lap. "Tell me how I can help you."

His eyes remained closed. She studied his face. He wasn't much older than she was, although his skin was a sickly gray. The boy's lips parted. "Put the totem around your neck. It will buy me a little time."

Emma stretched out her fingers and snatched the totem from the floor. She slipped it around her neck and the boy's ashen color warmed to an acorn brown.

"Now what?" she asked.

"There is nothing else you can do. My wounds are too great. But would you do me one favor?"

"Of course. Anything."

A spasm of pain appeared to rack his body and he grabbed at his ribs. "I want to know your name. I want to carry it on my lips when I pass to the spirit world."

Emma swallowed a lump in her throat. She could barely speak. "Emma," she whispered.

The boy flashed a weak smile. "Such a pretty name. Almost as pretty as your heart."

His breath rattled in his throat. Easing his head from her lap, Emma hurried to the sink for water. She dribbled the cool liquid between his swollen lips.

"Thank you," he said, weakly.

"It's the least I can do. You saved my life."

"No," he said, shaking his head. "I didn't mean for the water. For letting me be your protector. Now, when I hear the drums call, I can go knowing my life had a purpose. It will be a good death."

Emma choked back tears. "No, please, don't talk like that. You already look better."

"Don't be sad, Emma. I've lived many years, but now my wounds are too deep. It is my time."

"There has to be something I can do. I can go for help."

"No. There is only one way to save me, and it's impossible."

"What is it? Please tell me."

His eyes escaped her gaze and he grew quiet.

"Please!" Emma begged. "Tell me."

"I won't risk your life for mine. I've lived longer than any man should. My family is gone and it's time for me to join them."

"Tell me! Please, I have to know."

"Long ago," he said. "My family settled on land cursed by an ice-age shaman named Milak, an evil creature with an unyielding lust for destruction. He killed my folks and turned me into a wolf, a slave for the Ryan family. Weasel Tail was the last of them."

Emma cringed. "What a perfect name for that creep."

"There must be two totems recovered in order to save me. The first you wear around your neck. The second is hidden somewhere in the cursed land." Amarok coughed, clutched his sides and then continued. "Milak still haunts the valley and will transform anyone who dares to trespass. That is why I cannot risk your life."

"How much time do you have left?"

"One day, maybe two. The totem you wear will afford me more time."

"Where exactly is the other totem? Do you know?"

"Yes. It's somewhere on the grounds overlooking my parents' homestead."

"What does the other totem look like?"

"It's a twin to the one you wear, made from the tusk of a woolly mammoth. One controls my form; the other my life essence."

Emma fingered the totem, her distress so great that the item's tremendous age failed to rouse her interest. She got to her feet. "How far is it?"

Amarok pressed his lips together. "I don't want you to go."

"Please! Tell me!"

"I am supposed to protect you," he said, his smile weak. "I cannot ask this of you, the danger is too great. I couldn't bear the thought of you being enslaved by that creature. It is a hell beyond your imagining, a hell that no man, woman, or beast deserves." He took another gasping breath. "And there are wicked animals that guard that place, always on the lookout to do Milak's bidding."

"Look, I'm going to search for it either way. So you better tell me before we run out of time."

Amarok looked away.

"I have no one, except you." Emma's voice cracked. "My family is gone, too, and you're all I have left, so let me at least try. Please."

He frowned, opened his mouth to speak, and hesitated.

"Just tell me. If you don't, I'm going to start walking and hope I somehow find it. Either way, I'm going."

"All right," Amarok said. "I'll tell you, but you have to listen close. This isn't going to be easy. The quickest way is by kayak. There's a river a quarter of a mile from here. You'll see a trail. Follow the water downstream until you see an old cabin come into view. It's the only one near here that can be seen from the river. Promise me, Emma, that you won't take off that totem."

"I promise. I know that it gives you life as long as I wear it."

"No, that's not the only reason. If you wear it when you cross into the cursed land, Milak will not know you are there. He'll sense its presence and think it's Weasel Tail... unless he sees you. Take great care to stay out of his sight." He lifted his head, taking all his strength. "Please Emma, come back. Even if you don't save me, I want to see you again before I go... I don't want to die alone."

His eyes glistened with an intensity that made Emma's pulse race. His face was carved with high cheekbones and smooth skin and she found her eyes drawn to his full lips. Unconsciously, she touched her fingers to her mouth, wondering what his would feel like. She thought of how protected he'd made her feel when he stood in wolf form, defending her. She couldn't help but wonder how much nicer it would feel to have him offer that same protection with his human arms wrapped around her.

He touched her face and Emma closed her eyes.

"What you told me about... about your mother. It wasn't your fault," he whispered. His fingers traced her chin and she tilted her head into his touch until she felt her cheek cupped in his hand. She opened her eyes in surprise, fighting back tears. She'd told no one how she felt—except the wolf. Now she knew for certain that all of it was true. He *was* Amarok. He struggled to raise his upper body, reaching out to hold her, but his eyes filled with agony. Breaking the moment, Emma helped him lie back down on the floor.

"Let me get you a pillow and a warmer blanket. I'm going to leave some water where you can reach it." Emma gathered the items and placed the pillow under his head. She put the water near his hand and pulled the blankets up under his chin. She stroked his arm, and the feel of the smooth muscles made her heart leap.

He gazed at her in such a way that she felt a tightening in her chest, painful and thrilling at the same time. The way he looked at her with those piercing eyes pinned her to her spot. His eyes fluttered, and then closed. He let out a great sigh and slid into a fitful sleep.

22

Amarok lay in the silence, savoring the sound of Emma's name. Such a lovely name—it suited her. Her kindness had been a light, piercing the darkness of his weary soul, and her beautiful face shone like a dream in the stark reality of his existence. Would he ever see her again? His hand went to his cheek where she'd left a tender kiss before leaving. He imagined he could still feel the warmth of her touch and it thawed the frozen core that his heart had become. Her gentle caress had been the first touch he'd received in nearly a century that hadn't been harsh and brutal, and it was like a balm for wounds that ran deeper than his skin.

He only wished he could have opened his eyes and told her goodbye, but he was so tired. It didn't matter. She was still his girl; how could he have let her go? How could he have been so foolish as to let her risk her life? His life was over. She could never reach the cabin in time to save him. Even if she did find his totem, it would all be in vain. He'd be dead by the time she located it. He struggled to open his eyes, to make his body move, but his will was no match for the damage Suka had done, and the strength eluded him.

Amarok shivered. He was so terribly cold. The wool blanket and the roaring fire failed to chase away the bone-deep chill gripping him. Was death cold? He hoped not. He was so tired of being cold. It was tempting to let go, no longer to feel the bite of wintry freeze or the pain of his aberration of a life. But then Emma's image floated before his eyes, and he fought to live. His spirit would stay in his body for a while longer. He'd hold on for her.

He clenched his fist before his eyes, reveling in the hairless flesh. He'd mourned his human body over the years, missed it like a mother would a lost child. Even on the edge of death, with all the pain, it was rewarding to have it again, to feel with his fingers, to curl his toes, to lie on his side and feel the floor beneath him pressing into his skin. He ran his tongue over his teeth and smiled when it encountered human-sized canines. Amarok touched his face and wondered at the differences he'd felt in Emma's. He longed to smell her hair with a human nose, to hold her in his arms, to taste her lips… maybe in the next life, he'd get his chance.

His blood pulsed faintly, growing weaker. He closed his eyes, trying to shut out the drums overriding his heartbeat, the ancient death chant of his ancestors.

23

Emma carried the gun and a backpack, heavy with supplies. Her mind filled with doubt. Everything that had happened seemed too incredible to believe. A boy turned into a wolf? An evil shaman from the ice age? It all sounded crazy. How could any of this be real? But then it came to her, like light from a dark cloud—inside, somehow, she knew it was all too real. She'd seen it with her own eyes, cleaned his wounds with her own hands, and listened with her own ears to the strange tale.

Emma quickly followed the roar of rushing water north, down a mushy trail snaking around boulders and mossy trees. The path ended at a stony bank along a wide river. She studied the agitated water. The angry growl of the waves and the speed at which the river rushed made her stomach burn. She thought of her mother, lungs bursting with water, and her heart plummeted. Her throat felt dry, so she knelt on a smooth rock and drank from the frothy liquid. Emma savored the cold, coppery taste, swallowing down the horrible images of her dead mother.

A short way downstream, she spotted a kayak on the shore next to a crude wooden dock. Emma dragged the little boat as she climbed onto the structure, testing it first to make sure it wouldn't give way and plunge her into the icy river. The boards creaked and groaned under her weight, and with every step the water glugged and splashed onto her boots.

Emma set the double-bladed paddle on the dock. She wrapped the rope tied to the bow around her hand, slid the boat into the turbulent water, and attempted to get into the unsteady craft. The boat zipped from underneath her, and she jumped to the safety of the dock. She reeled the vessel in closer, pulling on the rope until the kayak rested against the pier. Emma found her footing and carefully climbed into the kayak. She clung to the dock with one hand, afraid of capsizing as she reached for the wooden paddle. Drawing in a deep breath, she pushed off with the paddle and guided the kayak into the swift water.

The current snagged her and she shot down the river at a frightening speed. Chunks of pack ice barreled past. She frantically alternated between steering and pushing them away from the sides of the fragile craft. The bitter wind sliced at her throat. She zipped the heavy parka higher, covering her mouth, and awkwardly pulled the ties on the waterproof skirt lining the opening of the kayak around her waist. The first wet flake of snow landed on her nose. "Perfect—just what I need!"

Emma laughed. She'd really done it this time. She'd gotten herself neck-deep in another mess. Trouble followed her like a predator after bleeding prey. But what did she have to lose by trying? Even if none of it were true—even if she'd lost her mind— man or wolf, Amarok was worth the struggle.

The river narrowed and she began to pick up even more speed, traveling faster and faster down the powerful current. Emma paddled hard, trying to gain control. The vessel keeled to one side, shooting into the middle fork of the waterway. Snow tumbled on the winds in thick smothering globs, muffling the sound of the rushing water and creating an eerie rumbling. Emma squinted, fighting to see as she barely missed a large rock, half-submerged in the foamy water. She paddled even harder, praying she'd regain control before her strength gave out. Finally, the river widened again and the waters slowed, giving her a rest from the breakneck speed.

Emma glanced at the dark trees, shrouded in snow like sheeted specters. Mountain men with guns and hideous monsters threatened her from every shadow. A bird screeched near her left ear and she almost sprang from the boat. Emma glanced upward as a huge owl slashed through the air, angled sideways, and landed somewhere in the tall trees ahead.

The bird's piercing eyes bored into hers as the kayak slid through the waves. Was it the same one that had been following Amarok? Could the thing be a spy for the shaman? The owl burst from the trees and swooped over her head. Emma shrieked and ducked. The owl wheeled, its big wings fanning the air, landing on the tip of the kayak. She studied the bird, a great snowy owl. She'd read about them in science class. Weren't they only out at night? Or was it during the day? The thing hopped closer and Emma gazed at its powder-white plumage, at the curious dark mark on its wing. The owl focused on Emma, letting out an alarming series of high-pitched shrieks. Something about its unsettling cries disturbed her, the way it seemed to see right into her soul, clacking its black beak like a bad omen.

Emma waved her paddle at it and the bird took flight, disappearing into brush along the bank. She kept her eyes on the spot, waiting for the owl to reappear, when something crashed out of the trees. Her chest tightened—timber wolves. Three snarling carnivores raced down the bank.

The boat slammed to a stop, entangled in the sunken branches of a log. The wolves leapt into the frigid waters, and Emma's heart seemed to leap from her chest as they approached. The lead wolf reached her first; it struggled to crawl into the boat, massive jaws snapping. Emma smashed at its head with the paddle. The beast gave a yelp of pain and sank into the icy depths, and then surfaced near the bank. The other wolves thrashed in the water, the freezing temperatures stealing their speed.

Emma shoved the paddle down hard and pushed against the log, freeing the boat. A second wolf climbed onto the bow of the kayak, pushing it dangerously low in the water. The creature lost its footing, yelped, and slipped off.

She paddled into the current, continuing the perilous trek downriver, every nerve on high alert. Another fork in the river appeared dead ahead. Making a quick decision, she paddled to the right and instantly regretted it. The arctic water roiled beneath the vessel. More snags and log jams clogged the route. Treacherous rocks scraped along her hull.

The boat picked up speed and a deafening roar thundered in her ears. She nearly fainted as she spotted the massive drop-off. Tucking the paddle under one arm, Emma gripped the sides of the boat, holding on with all her strength. The kayak flew over the ledge and went airborne for one terrifying moment before it slammed back into the water. Jagged rocks protruded like knives in every direction. Emma screamed as the kayak flipped, dumping her out of the boat and into the river.

The freezing water took hold of her like a skeletal hand closing around her throat. The current wrapped icy fingers around her ankles, pulling her under. She fought to the surface, but just before she reached it, her muscles went numb. She flailed her arms until her fingers raked across a rocky outcropping. Emma lost her grip and sank into the murky depths. So cold. So dark. She spiraled downward, kicking and twisting to get back to the surface. Something tangled around her boots. What's down there? Her muscles grew heavier, cramping. God, no!

She burst to the surface. The cold air seized her chest. She sank again, surfaced and saw a man reaching for her, just as she went under again. His face old and leathery, he smiled with piercing brown eyes, stirred the waters beneath her, and sucked her down into the unknown. Her mind embraced one last terrifying thought—how easily the shaman had killed her.

24

The fire winked and faded into glowing embers. Chills racked Amarok's battered frame. His thoughts turned to Emma, alone in the cold. She never should have gone on such a dangerous journey by herself. His spirit ached to go to her, her pull stronger than the drums that continued to haunt him, but his body remained stubbornly unresponsive. He couldn't even crawl to what remained of the fire to protect himself from the cold. How could he protect her? The instinct was so strong that, if still in wolf form, he would've howled his frustration.

This was all his fault. He should have lied to her, sent to her Ben's place. The kindly trapper would have seen to her safety. But in his pain and desperation, he hadn't thought quickly enough. Now, it was too late. He'd put Emma in harm's way. What if—no! He couldn't bear the thought of her being transformed into some kind of beast, enslaved forever, her love for him slowly changing to resentment and then hatred with the knowledge that it'd been his fault. Her humanity gradually eaten away as her rage turned her into a monster to be feared, rather than a girl to be loved. Tears, the first he'd shed in longer than he could remember, slid from his eyes. If only he'd been strong enough. He was supposed to protect her, and instead he'd condemned her to the life that had nearly driven him mad.

He clenched his fists. Everything and everyone he'd ever cared about had fallen victim to Milak's evil—first his family, and now the girl he'd grown so fond of. He rubbed his feverish forehead and the touch of his own hand soothed him. He remembered how Emma had stroked his fur so gently, and then touched his arm as a man. Amarok smiled, remembering how she had gazed at him. Had he really seen affection in her eyes, or had he simply imagined it? Please, let it be true. He struggled to sit upright. Pain ripped through him. He clutched his sides. What good would love do him now? He'd be dead before she returned. If she did come back. Tears burned his eyes. He breathed deeply, trying to calm himself. He thought of his father, and what he'd say if he saw his son behaving like this. He bit back his tears and forced himself to allow a faint glimmer of hope into his heart. What if, by some miracle, she found the second totem in time? He would live again! But would she stay with him, out here in the middle of nowhere? Maybe she'd leave him for the city, and perhaps that was the right thing to do. If he left this area, he would age and die in a matter of days. The Ryans had taken sadistic pleasure in reminding him of that. He put all thoughts out of his mind and gazed into the gaping mouth of the hearth. It waited, empty and cold, like his life without Emma.

A loud tap shattered his sad thoughts. The tap came again and again.

Coming from the window.

25

Can't breathe! Emma kicked and flailed in the frigid water until she twisted enough to fling the suffocating wool blanket from her body. She jolted awake. Where was she? She spotted an old native sitting across from her, his face a map of wrinkles, dark eyes peering into hers. Every muscle trembled.

"Who are you?" Emma asked.

The man smiled and put his hand up. "My name's Ben, and you're lucky I checked my trap lines when I did. You darn near froze to death."

Emma glanced around the modest cabin, fighting the urge to rush out the door. A small kitchen sat just off the living room. Wooden shelves lined the walls, stocked with plates and napkins. A round table stood in the middle of the room, a deck of playing cards fanned out across the center. It didn't look like the dwelling of an ice age shaman.

She quivered uncontrollably, her teeth chattering hard enough to break. Even sitting in front of the man's fire, Emma shivered.

The trapper gestured to a flannel shirt and a pair of camouflage pants. "You best get out of those wet clothes. If you hadn't woken, I was going to strip you down myself before hypothermia set in. Those are my wife's clothes, but you can have them. She doesn't like it out here and rarely visits. If you don't mind me asking… what are you doing out here by yourself?"

Emma grabbed for the totem and felt the comfortable thump of it against her chest.

"I have a friend who's in trouble, and he needs me."

The man shook his head. "And you need to find the twin to that totem you wear around your neck to help this friend… right?"

Emma gasped. "How did you know?"

"An old legend told in my tribe when I was a kid. I always suspected there was truth to it. I hate that bastard Weasel Tail, and I hate the way he treats his animals even worse. He likes to steal from my trap lines."

"He won't be stealing anything anymore. He's dead."

The man sat bolt upright, his brows arched in surprise. Had she said too much? Would he drag her to the authorities before she could save Amarok?

"He was mauled by a bear."

The trapper's mouth twisted into a humorless smile and his eyes glinted. "There won't be anyone to mourn his passing. Lots of folks will breathe easier knowing he's gone. I know I will."

A teakettle whistled. Ben motioned toward the kitchen. "I'll make you something to drink. It will help warm you up."

"No thanks." Emma forced herself her to her feet. "I really need to get going. I have to get back to my friend."

"This friend of yours, is he a wolf?"

Emma nodded and the man walked to a far closet. He tossed her a heavy parka and handed her the pack she'd been wearing when he dragged her from the water.

"You'll need a ride, then," Ben said. "I can take you where you need to go, but I won't set foot on that land. I saved your firearm, but I couldn't save the kayak. I'll give you one hour to look, and then I'm leaving. We can take my boat."

26

The tapping became more insistent, louder, shaking the window panes. Amarok squeezed his eyes shut and covered his ears to block the sound out, but it become so loud he could feel its vibrations.

"No!" Amarok gritted his teeth. "You're dead!" He squeezed his eyes tighter and clenched his jaw. How could Weasel Tail have survived? It wasn't possible! But, if he had… and if he somehow gained his strength back, he'd hunt Emma to the death. Amarok turned his fevered head and stared at the window, the worst possible scenarios jabbing into his brain. He struggled to focus on the source of the noise, but snow fell outside and the brightness, combined with the distorting frost, made it hard to distinguish shapes. A dark shadow loomed and his heart skipped. Maybe it was Emma. His mind grasped at thin shreds of hope, fighting back the fear growing inside him. Maybe she was hurt and needed him! He pulled his way along the floor to lie beneath the window frame, every movement feeling as if he'd ripped open a dozen new wounds. Dragging himself up to look, his breath caught in his throat as he stared into a pair of yellow eyes.

Amarok frowned, it wasn't possible. Or was it? He gazed at the thing resting on his windowsill, peering at him through the dusty glass. Was it just his mind, wanting to conjure up some kind of miracle?

But then a shimmering splinter pierced the darkness and he allowed himself to believe in the impossible. His heart jumped. Could it really be?

27

Emma sat in the bow of the motorboat, straining to see past the flying snow as they traveled downstream. Even after changing into dry clothes, she still shivered from the bitter wind. She surveyed the gloomy landscape, glad to have a guide to show her the way. Fingering the totem, Emma's heart twisted with worry for Amarok. Was he still alive? *Please, just hang on.* Her stomach clenched—she couldn't handle another death. No matter how she tried, she couldn't shake the restlessness inside, the horrible fear that made her legs tremble. She'd never been afraid of anything, not until now. If she screwed this up, there'd be no second chances.

Emma clung to the edge of the boat until her fingers went numb. The undulating rumble of the boat motor slowed as they maneuvered around dead logs and debris clogging the route. Emma glanced at Ben. His brown eyes made uneasy sweeps of the shoreline. The deeper they traveled downriver, the colder it got, dropping at least ten degrees every mile.

Angry clouds painted the sky a threatening shade of smokestack gray, a dark mirror of the landscape below. Flat slabs of granite lined the riverbank, standing like tombstones over rotten logs floating like corpses in the freezing water. Dead fish echoed the graveyard impression, lying in a spray of guts and bones on the frozen bank.

They rounded a bend and she spotted the outline of an old cabin on a knoll overlooking the river, exactly as Amarok had described it. Ben eased up on the throttle and edged the vessel toward the bank.

She turned to Ben. "Wow, I can't believe the cabin is still standing."

He nodded, his voice dropping. "Things don't seem to age here, like they do in the rest of the world."

Emma shivered, cradling the gun in her lap. Maybe that was why the shaman had been able to survive for so many centuries. The boat bumped into the shore, and Emma leaned over and tied it to a limb sticking out of the embankment. She balanced precariously in the belly of the ship and then, summoning up her courage, made a giant leap for the shore. The boat shot out from under her feet and snapped to the end of its tether, but she cleared the shallow water and landed on the mucky edge of the sandbank. She glanced at Ben, who pointed to his watch and waved her onward. Emma barreled into the thick foliage. One hour, that's all she had before he'd leave her. Adrenaline surged, igniting the blood in her veins. She had to hurry.

Emma pushed her way through a clump of tall, stiff cattails to a narrow trail made by a large animal with cloven hooves— probably moose or elk. Thorns, under a shield of snow, gored at her exposed face, and shrubs with poking branches stabbed at her legs. She labored ahead, fighting slushy pools of water and muck to a stone footpath leading to the cabin. The structure's huge, notched logs remained standing, a testament to the quality of their workmanship.

An unexpected wave of sadness washed over her. Such a lonely spot to build a home. She saw the remains of flower boxes under the windows, rotting into the earth. Two weathered crosses leaned at odd angles behind the house, as if placed by a drunken hand. They stood as the only reminders of the lives of those who lay beneath them—a family destroyed, dreams decomposing into the earth.

She ducked into the weatherbeaten little house. Rat urine and the stench of musty wood assaulted her nostrils. Emma glanced around the shadowy interior. Three iron bed frames stood pushed against the walls, their mattresses and support ropes having long since fallen victim to time and generations of rodents. Tin plates and dusty cups sat on a board nailed into a log wall.

Emma crossed the room to a cracked window. Something furry and brown scuttled under her feet. She choked down a scream as a huge rat slid under the crumbling doorframe, making its escape. Using the side of her fist, she cleared a dusty spot away and peered outside. Emma's gaze swept across the barren terrain to a mountain overlooking the cabin. Her heart jumped. Something about the hillside made her uneasy. It set off an internal instinct telling her to flee, to get away while she still could, before it was too late. Her thoughts returned to Amarok and she squared her shoulders. The last thing she would do was give up. She would not let the darkness win.

She fingered the totem around her neck, making sure it was still there. She eyed it carefully, memorizing every detail, staring into the center of it, as if she could will it to reveal the hiding place of its twin. Emma frowned. It had to be nearby, but where? Milak would have hidden it well. She chewed her lower lip. If it were buried years ago, how would she be able to find it now, after all this time? Emma's legs wobbled; she needed to sit down. It all seemed so impossible. She suddenly couldn't breathe, and her heart threatened to punch through her chest. She felt herself starting to disconnect. *No, Em, not this time—not now!* She drew in one calming breath after another until her racing pulse returned to normal. Disconnecting didn't do any good. Cutting solved nothing. She had to face what had to be done. The cool caress of the blade and her dizzying escapes into her own mind only distracted her for a short time. They did nothing to remove those parts of her life she least wanted to face. No matter what, she would find the totem—she refused to let Amarok die.

Her mind raced. She'd have to hurry; she didn't have much time. She'd stick to the tree line, keep herself hidden, and check out the hillside and surrounding area.

She headed out the back but suddenly stopped. At her feet, Emma spotted a faded tobacco tin covered in cobwebs. Something about it drew her to it. Thinking that it might hold some kind of clue, she brushed the sticky webbing away, picked it up and took it to the window for more light. Lifting the lid, she peered inside.

28

Amarok studied the creature's wing and his heart froze. Could it be? Though blurred by the texture of feathers and lacking the intricate detail of the original, the mark was immediately recognizable. The bird flew off and then returned as if silently trying to communicate with him, telling him he was not alone. Amarok knew who the bird was. It explained so much, but if he'd been captive all this time, how had he gotten free? And how long had he been hiding?

Amarok closed his eyes; his body couldn't take much more. He struggled to catch his breath and lie still on the hard floor that pressed into his bones. Memories of the owner of the mark came flooding back, and he explored a time in his life before this wretched existence. He'd been eight years old when he'd first met his father's brother. Uncle Jock had stood over six feet tall, with the length of two axe handles across his broad back. Winter-lean and muscle-bound, he'd been an Adonis to young ladies and an idol to adolescent boys. But no one idolized Jock more than Amarok, and when his family had left Canada, his strapping uncle had promised to follow close behind.

True to his word, Jock had come to Alaska soon after, but he'd preferred the life of a fisherman to that of a prospector or trapper. While Tok and his family headed to the cursed lands, Jock settled near the ocean and the pubs of town. On one burly bicep, Jock had worn a tattoo of a bird—an owl in flight—so if he were ever lost at sea and his body drifted to shore, he'd be identifiable.

One golden September day, Amarok had received a letter from his favorite uncle. Jock was coming to get him. He was to spend two glorious months at sea with his idol. The life of a fisherman seemed exciting and mysterious, compared to the tedium of walking trap lines. On the day Jock was to arrive, Amarok had woken early and nearly worn a path in the floor from checking the window for signs of Jock. By nightfall, all hopes of seeing his uncle were dashed. Day after day, he watched and waited, praying for any sign of the big man. But when the autumn leaves fell and snow covered the ground, Amarok gave up hope. As weeks passed with no word from the big man, Amarok's father grimly concluded his brother was gone, lost to some unnamed danger.

Now, Amarok knew differently. Somehow, the old shaman had captured Jock and turned him into an owl—the very owl perched on his windowsill, and the same one that had followed him across the tundra. He'd even given the girl a silver feather from its plumage.

If only he could stand and get to the door, he'd let him in. It would comfort to him to have Jock at his side. Through all the years, everyone he'd known had died. Now, here was the uncle he'd loved like a father, alive and well. Not in human form, as he would have wanted, but alive nonetheless.

Amarok thought back to the time the shaman had transformed him, to the days when he'd lain in agony while the transformation had taken place. During those nights, he'd heard the beat of wings against the hut and the screeches of a bird. Could it have been his uncle trying to save him? And, slowly, he recalled seeing an owl on the arm of the old shaman when his first master, Abe, had come for him. More than once, a lonesome hoot had broken the silence of the long, cold nights.

An arrow of doubt shot through his veins like lead. Had he imagined it all? Had he really seen the mark on the bird's wing? Was it just his dying mind giving him comfort? Amarok closed his eyes, refusing to not believe in what he had seen. After all the years of needless suffering, this one thing had to be true. *Please, let it be so.*

As Amarok struggled to sit up, a sharp pain flashed through his side. He put his hand on his waist, feeling blood seep through his bandages. He made his agonizing way to the cold hearth. With his remaining strength, he stoked the fire into a blaze and collapsed on the bed.

It'd been years since he'd slept within the shelter of four walls and a warm fire. Amarok soaked in the warmth, staring at the flames licking the wood, devouring it. He thought of all the other people enslaved by Milak, their lives destroyed. Something dreadful occurred to him. If Milak was as old as the ice age, then perhaps there were others who'd lived centuries in slavery. Amarok clamped his eyes shut. He couldn't imagine such a horrible thing.

29

Emma peered into the metal box. Underneath an antique pocket watch and three gold coins, she spotted a hardbound book. On the cracked leather of the spine, the word "Journal" was stamped in gold lettering. She reached inside and gently eased it out. Carefully, Emma leafed through the musty pages. Most were unreadable, smeared with specks of mold. She flipped to the last entry.

January 21, 1865

I've grown sicker by the day. My vision is so poor I can hardly see to write this entry. The native tales of cursed lands and ill fortune ring true. I saw the evil one with my own eyes, and in his hateful glare he cursed me with a terrible blight that has taken over my body. I fear for my wife and son. Beware all those who near his mountain, for inside it lies not a man, but a terrible monster.

Louis Baptise

Emma shivered and closed the fragile diary, returning it to the box. She glanced out the window at the mountain, eyeing its dark, oppressive peaks. A terrible dread filled her gut—somewhere deep within those rocky folds, the shaman hid. Maybe he already knew she was there, and so was watching and waiting for her. Either way, it didn't matter. She was going to get Amarok's totem, and nothing would stand in her way. Determination steeled her spine; she pushed open the door and headed out. Emma hiked from the cabin up a set of barren hills toward the base of the mountain. She adjusted the heavy pack, keeping the massive landmark in focus. Something about it repulsed her, made her feel cold and unclean, and she fought the urge to turn back. The unsettling feelings only confirmed her belief that this was where the shaman resided, as if his presence had corrupted the place, permeating even the rock with his evil. She lumbered through patches of dead grass and slush, her footsteps the only sound.

Emma kept to the trees, trying to remain hidden. The back of her neck prickled. All the while, she felt eyes watching her from every angle. She glanced around. Branches snapped behind her and she paused. Her pulse hammered in her ears, an unswallowable knot forming in her throat. She took two more steps, and the shuffle of feet crunched behind her. She whirled, holding the gun high, scanning the land around her. No one— not one sound. She continued a few yards, until a shrill scream broke the silence. Emma froze, unable to move her feet, her heart punching into her ribcage. *What the hell was that?* She waited a minute, then two, but no threat materialized. She worked her way up and up, peering over her shoulder all the while to make sure she wasn't being followed. A few steps later, she reached the base of the mountain.

Emma scanned its heights and focused on a high eave. Behind it, a yawning cave punctured the granite. The rocky surface angled upward from the ground to the cave ledge, making an imperfect set of steps.

She leaned face-first against the icy wall, inhaling the pungent odors of sage and moss. Using her fingertips, she grasped at tiny protruding ledges, pulling herself up. The weight of the backpack caused the straps to bite into her shoulders. Emma winced, sweat beading her forehead. Gritting her teeth, she climbed higher, muscles screaming, until she reached the lip of the cornice and peered over the top. Loose shale and scattered twigs cluttered the surface. She hauled herself up onto the broad ledge and shrugged off the pack, surveying the sweeping valley below.

Emma peered down at Amarok's old cabin. She wrapped her arms around herself as an unsettling thought occurred to her. She could see into the windows. Her stomach knotted, thinking how the shaman must have stalked the family, watching and waiting for just the right time to unleash his deadly curse, keeping himself coiled, like a venomous snake, in the shadows.

Emma filled her lungs with cold mountain air, trying to take the edge off her agitated nerves. She eyed the cave opening and slipped on her pack. Moss clung to the vertical limestone walls, and an eerie fog hovered in the void between the floor and ceiling.

Her scalp tingled. What if she ran into a bear or disturbed a nest of bats? She shuddered. An animal encounter would be better than one with the shaman. She could feel his evil presence seeping out of the walls, a presence so strong she could hardly breathe.

Emma peered into the cave, her gaze swallowed by the impenetrable blackness. She took a step inside, senses on high alert. She clutched the rifle until her knuckles burned. Clicking the flashlight on, she took another step. The clammy interior exhaled a musty breeze, chilling its way into her bones.

She fought to focus in the haze, seeing tiny flicks of lights appear, then fade into nothing. Emma took another wary step. Something crunched beneath her boots. A chill sliced up her spine. She shone a beam of light over the floor. Hundreds of dead beetles lay scattered on their backs. Bones of all sizes lay strewn across the flowstone on brown stains of dried blood, like a slaughterhouse floor. She closed her eyes and swallowed hard, fighting the urge to gag.

Emma steadied herself, stepped inside, and let the darkness swallow her.

30

The windowsill stood cold and barren, empty of life and love. Amarok rested on the floor, listening for any sounds of the owl's return. Once in a while, he would see the glint of falling snow, or hear the shrill of squirrels preparing their dens for winter, and his pulse would race. How hard it was to just lie there, helpless, worthless. So utterly alone.

Amarok's thoughts returned, time and time again, to Emma. He tried to console himself, convince himself, that his uncle would protect her. But what could a bird do? Hope struggled for a foothold. Maybe, if nothing else, he could guide her to where the totem lay hidden, if she made it that far. The need to believe she was out of harm's way warred with the knowledge of what she faced, and his head began to pound. It seemed like days since her departure instead of hours. Her absence left a hollow emptiness in his very existence.

A violent wave of fear stabbed through Amarok's spine. So many dangers lay ahead of her—the river, the plunging temperature, wild animals and, worst of all, Milak himself.

Amarok closed his eyes, attempting to push the terrible thoughts from his mind. He tried to visualize what life might be like if Emma returned with the totems. His eyelids flew open, and he released a heavy sigh. He knew better than to humor such outlandish ideas, but somehow, it made the pain of his wounds almost bearable.

Emma deserved to have someone to care for her, to love her. It wasn't right for her to be left all alone, with no one to protect her.

He only wished that somehow, he could be the one at her side, but time was his enemy and he feared the endless sleep would take him before he even had a chance to see her once more.

31

Emma stumbled through the dark, following the faint beam of her flashlight. Shale and bits of gravel rolled from beneath her boots. The rocks scattered ahead and disappeared with a loud splash. She jerked to a stop, shining the flashlight along the stone floor. Inches from her feet, an enormous sinkhole punctured the ground. Emma sucked in a breath, staring down into the watery pit. One or two more steps, and she would've plunged into a boggy grave. She had to keep her wits about her, even though she was painfully aware of the minutes ticking away. Being careless would cost her more than time. Slow and cautious was better than quick and dead.

She eased her way around the gaping hole and entered a wide chamber. Jagged stalactites, like stone daggers, hung from the ceiling. Foul water dripped down their sharp blades into deep, scummy ponds. A narrow trail wove among them.

A putrid scent of decay seeped from the walls. Emma fought to stay on the narrow path. She stumbled and stepped ankle-deep into one of the murky puddles, almost losing her boot in the sucking mud. She pulled her foot loose and pushed on. Around a tight bend, Emma came to a massive entranceway, braced on each side by a giant tusk and topped with a massive skull. She waved the flashlight over the colossal skeleton of what must have been a mammoth. Deep etchings of interlacing circles and arrows marred the bone surfaces. Her pulse quickened. *This has to be the right way!*

Emma ducked under the skull, passing dark intersections, tunnels, and chasms. Niches of blackness filled with strange sounds made her glad she didn't know what lurked inside. Palms sweating, she ventured deeper and deeper into the unsettling cave. Her flashlight shone a weak path into the darkness, illuminating a segment of tunnels. *Which way?* Emma studied the four catacombs and selected the largest.

The tunnel angled downward, and with every step, Emma's throat tightened. Something gleamed from the walls. She held the flashlight close to the stony surface. The beam flickered across faded brush strokes. Muted reds and blacks depicted animals, men, and beasts. One figure stood out in the middle, a giant god-like creature with horns on his head and fur robes draped over his shoulders. At his feet half-men, half-beasts twisted in misery.

Darkness wound around her, smothering all but the faint beam of her flashlight and shrouding her in panic. Panic shot through her veins. She had to get out—now. Her head spun with terrifying thoughts. She didn't want to die here, her soul trapped forever. Clenching her jaw, she fought the urge to escape the unholy place. She pressed ahead, forcing herself to go deeper into the dark and dangerous unknown.

The flashlight winked and faded out. Emma froze. She shook it hard until the batteries nearly fell out. The light flickered, then came on. Fear slithered down her spine. If the light went out for good, she'd be trapped, alone in the dark, stumbling through a dangerous maze. The flashlight flickered again. Emma smacked it against the stone wall. The beam clicked on as wings flapped and the air filled with horrible screeching. She looked up in time to see an army of bats descending from the ceiling. She dropped to the floor and covered her head. *Don't scream, don't...*

They flew off in a bunch and Emma stood, listening to their leathery wings snapping into the dark. She held the light in front of her, forging ahead, entering another large chamber, taking stock of the room, praying the commotion of the bats hadn't alerted the shaman to her presence. The enormous cavern resembled a tomb, with stalagmites for monuments. The flashlight played over the pools of stagnant water, reflecting like stained glass.

A granite altar dominated the center of the room. Suspended from the ceiling, stalks of dried plants hung like dozens of skeletal fingers. Beyond the stone shrine, Emma spied a flash of bleached bone. Her light revealed the ancient ribcage of an enormous beast. From each rib hung a totem. She ran over, searching through the maze of carved animals. She found bears, raccoons, birds, snakes and rabbits. Her heart sank. How many people had been enslaved by this monster? Emma gritted her teeth and snatched the totems one by one, searching for Amarok's. Only two totems left. One had to be the one she needed. She grabbed the first one. In the dim light she saw the outline of wolf ears. Her breath caught in her throat. She'd found it! She held it to the light, and her shoulders sagged. A fox. She slipped it into her backpack and reached for the last one. This had to be it... *please!* She snatched the last totem—a wolf, yes!—and slipped it around her neck.

Footsteps shuffled behind her. Emma froze, listening so hard she could hear the air filtering in through tiny cracks in the walls. Another shuffle.

Louder.

Closer.

32

Something awoke Amarok, but he couldn't say what. The blood seeping through his bandages slowed, and the haze in his eyes cleared. His body still ached and with every move, the cuts raking across his frame continued to burn like fire, but something was different—very different.

His heart swelled. Was it possible? Had Emma found his totem? He laid his head down and rolled onto his back, staring at the ceiling. If it were true and he was really going to survive, the first thing he had to do was make sure Emma was safe, and then he would free the others from Milak's spell. If he could find their totems and reunite them, the curse would be broken. He thought of Suka, and a shiver penetrated his heart. If the bear were still alive, what would he be like now, as a man? As an animal, he was a mindless killing machine fueled by rage. Would he continue his bloody reign in human form? Amarok hated the thought of sharing a forest with that sort of madness, whether he was man or beast.

The thought of Suka brought more questions. He knew he could never leave the cursed lands or he'd age and die within a few days. But how long would Emma want to stay in such seclusion? Would she run off to the city? Could he make her so insanely happy that she'd never want to leave? It didn't matter; he knew it would be wrong to try. She had a real life to lead, not the primitive and isolated existence that was all he had to offer. His shoulders sagged. It all seemed so impossible.

He loved the idea of living again as a man and it filled him with happiness, but still, a part of his heart ached. He couldn't stand the thought of losing Emma. What good was it to live if he were totally alone, bound to a land void of everyone he'd ever loved and unable to follow them?

He'd thought being trapped in the body of a wolf had been the loneliest existence possible. He'd been wrong. It wasn't being unable to speak. It hadn't even been suffering from starvation and physical abuse. It was being denied love and companionship. If he freed the others, he might find friendship and camaraderie, but if Emma left, love would be beyond his grasp.

33

Emma bolted from the chamber, flashlight jiggling in her hand as she ran. It illuminated flashes of random horror around her, like a strobe light in a haunted house. The murmur of chanting echoed off the cave walls, bouncing back as if it were coming from every crevice, every dark nook. The awkward weight of the backpack threw her off-balance and she nearly lost her footing more than once. If she hadn't put all the totems inside it, she would have ditched it by now.

Her boots slapped across the flowstone, adding an eerie rhythm to the voice booming around her. She skidded past a corner and into the next chamber, grasping at mossy stone and who knew what else, to help her keep her balance. The chanting grew louder, seeming to rise and fall, a frightening counterpoint to her pounding heart.

Swords of daylight speared into the dark from the cave's yawning entrance. Emma's pulse picked up a notch. Just a few more steps, and she'd reach freedom. The chanting turned into a yowl as she burst from the dark cave into daylight. A powerful wind shrieked, lashing at her back. It wrapped sharp talons around her ankles. Emma tripped and fell. She tasted blood, scrambled to her feet and fell again. The pull increased. She kicked at the hands, looking at her legs as her feet met no resistance. Behind her, traces of mist seemed to gain substance as it tried to drag her into the darkness.

A shadow fell over the rocky lip. She shot a glance upward. An owl swooped low and ripped the totems from her neck. It launched into the sky again, dropping bits of rotten leather behind.

"No!" Emma screamed, flipping onto her back, kicking harder at the nothingness that held her. The grip tightened, pulling her along the cold, wet floor. She managed to flip onto her belly again. Her fingernails ripped as she frantically clawed stone, seeking a finger-hold to buy more time. The thing had dragged her halfway inside when an alarming hum echoed in the distance. A boat motor.

Her blood froze.

Ben was leaving her.

34

With every breath, strength slowly flowed into Amarok's battered body. How was it possible? He'd lain here for hours in the clutches of death and now suddenly, the reaper had lost his grip. Granted, every muscle still ached, and the wounds covering his body were just as excruciating, but something had changed. It was the pain of a wounded man, not a dying one. He inhaled deeply for the first time in hours, and his vision cleared.

It could only mean one thing. Emma had found the twin to his totem! Somehow, she'd done it and now he was soon to be free—forever. For the magic to be this powerful, she had to be somewhere close. He crawled his way to the door and opened it. *Please, dear God, allow me this one bit of happiness. This one miracle.*

A sudden shift in the wind alerted him and Amarok looked up as an enormous owl drifted in through the opening on silent wings. It landed on his hip, the black talons digging in painfully, threatening to tear even more flesh until it hopped to the floor.

From its wicked-looking black beak hung the two totems. Amarok's eyes widened in stunned disbelief. He reached out and grabbed the totems, draping them around his neck. His gaze shot to the door, but Emma didn't appear. He frowned at the owl.

"Where's Emma?"

The owl cocked its head and regarded him with hooded yellow eyes. Then it launched itself into the air, the backdraft of the gigantic wings fanning over him. The bird escaped out the door, only to land at the edge of the clearing, waiting. Suddenly, he understood. Emma had been captured, and Uncle Jock was showing him the way. He struggled to stand. His muscles were unfamiliar in his true form, and his near brush with death had left him weak. Although he managed to get up again, he only took a single step before losing his balance and falling. He wobbled like a newborn fawn taking its first steps. He'd have to relearn how to walk upright like a man, but he had no time to practice. Amarok grabbed onto a chair for support and tried again. His knuckles turned white as he held on. He took two steps and collapsed in a heap.

He slammed a fist into the floor, rose to his knees, and then to his feet once more. It had been so long since he'd stood as a man—almost too long to remember. He dragged himself into the chair and flexed his ankles, feeling his flesh tingle. Amarok took a deep breath to steady himself, determination thick in his veins, and he stood again. His muscles went into painful spasms and he shuffled until he could bear the weight without falling.

Amarok took another step forward, focused on planting one foot in front of the other. He stretched his memory back to when he'd been a teenager running along the sandy riverbank, when his legs had ached from long, difficult hikes with his father. What a beautiful sensation to stand, but he'd take the time to enjoy it later. Right now, Emma needed him.

Underneath Weasel Tail's bed, he found a pair of long johns and wool pants, socks and a plaid shirt. He'd still need boots and a gun. Amarok searched the room. He'd only seen the man with one pair of shoes. Hobbling to the door, he peered out at Weasel Tail's lifeless frame. Amarok choked down a wave of disgust. The man was already turning back into some sort of beast, his body sprouting a thick coat of gray fur, his features twisting and distorting as he started to decompose. Amarok stepped into the snow, the cold burning his bare feet. He knelt and quickly unlaced the man's boots, and then pried the gun from his rigid hands.

Amarok hurried inside, drying his freezing feet before slipping on the socks and boots. He looked around desperately; an empty gun was nothing more than a club. Suka was still out there somewhere. He could sense the beast nearby, waiting to attack. Amarok knew Weasel Tail would have used his gun to force his way inside, if there had been any shells in it. His stomach clenched. Emma had taken the last of the ammo. He didn't have time to hike to Weasel Tail's cache for more. The bear would smell the blood from his wounds and he'd be easy prey. He'd have to move fast. He tossed the useless weapon onto the bed. Emma had risked her life to save his. He didn't want to die, not now, not after all this. But if that's what it took to save her, he'd gladly do so.

35

Emma awoke slowly, caught up in the disorientation of waking in a strange place. She stared up at a ceiling of bones and hides as her mind struggled to interpret what she saw. Where was she? She rolled onto her side, her body complaining with each movement. Pungent smells swirled around her—dampness, fungus, decay.

A shroud of ice fog surrounded her like a veil of gauze. The thump of drums and the skirl of chanting swirled from within its murky depths. A swelling fear engulfed her, as her memory came pouring back. The chanting, the cave, all of it flooded her terrified mind. Emma sucked in a frightened gasp, struggling to sit up, paralyzed by the haunting rhythm. She gawked in wide-eyed horror at the source of the terrible sound. A hunched figure, barely discernible, crouched in the icy mist. A smug smile cracked across a brittle face dominated by a huge, jutting forehead above wrinkly eyes. Misshapen, black teeth gleamed in the torchlight, a forked tongue darting between them.

Emma opened her mouth to scream, but terror strangled her vocal cords. The shaman threw back his head and laughed, shaking a set of rattles, spiraling around her. She clamped her eyes shut, trying to close out the sounds, fighting the burning pain searing her skin. Emma remembered the lost totems. Bitter tears sprang to her eyes. She tried to raise a hand to wipe her face, but every limb felt weighed down by blocks of stone. With an overpowering certainty, she knew what the old man was doing. She'd risked everything to free Amarok and instead, she'd experience the half-life he'd lived for so long. Very soon, she'd be transformed into an animal with a human mind, trapped forever.

The chanting and rattling intensified, sending shards of pain slicing into her head. The horrible pressure bulged behind her sinuses. Her temperature spiked, yet her body shook with chills. He was trying to make her sick, invade her mind—weaken her spirit. Emma twisted and contorted in agony, feeling her bones soften, her tissues expand. Light exploded behind her eye sockets and she feared they would burst from her head.

Anger and pain collided inside of her, only to be replaced with cold conviction. She clenched her teeth until her molars ached. Emma knew how to beat him. She'd use one of her worst habits; something she fought constantly, but would now be to her advantage. Emma inhaled deeply and let herself drift away…

36

Amarok hurried from the cabin, struggling to get used to the feeling of being vertical. His steps were slow and stilted at first, but his skill and confidence increased with each moment. Amarok's heart pumped with exhilaration as his soul ascended new heights. He would find Emma, and nothing would get in his way.

His boots churned up bits of soggy moss and ferns with his slow, lumbering pace. At the foot of the path, the cramps assaulting his calves ceased. He paused to rest, watching angry thunderheads churn from gray to black, fertile with burdensome bellies of rain. He didn't have much time before the storm blew inland, soaking the land in sheets of freezing precipitation, encapsulating the forest in a cold and impenetrable ice-bound prison. The rivers would rise with the rain, making travel even more treacherous.

Amarok stumbled along the rocky path to the river. The scent of fermented moss berries, mulch, and cedar flavored the air with a musky tang. Drifts of heavy snow already littered the water's edge in a ring of white. He glanced at the dock, his clothes damp with perspiration. How could he have forgotten? Emma had taken the kayak. He'd have to hike to Ben's place north of the river, an impossible feat. An uphill climb across some of the roughest terrain in the area, and he was a century out of practice.

Knotting his fists, Amarok kicked a rock into the middle of the river. It would take him a full day or longer to get there, and there was no guarantee the trapper would be home. A skilled bush pilot, Ben transported hunters and tourists around remote areas of the Alaskan frontier. Weasel Tail had known Ben's schedule. He'd wait, lurking in the brush until Ben left, and while the trapper was gone, Weasel Tail would raid his traps. Amarok suddenly remembered a beat-up canoe stored in a southern cache. It would be only a short hike, but repairs would take half a day.

A motor whined in the distance, breaking his concentration. The drone grew louder and stronger. Upriver, the outline of Ben's boat came into view. Amarok waved his hands to get the man's attention. He watched as the vessel drew near and he spotted the trapper's face. Ben appeared ashen, his lips pressed tight. He slowed and idled to the dock, watching Amarok with suspicious eyes.

"Thank God—Ben! You have to take me to the dark valley before it's too late."

Ben lifted his chin, and squinted. "Do I know you?"

"Please, just listen to me. I need a ride downriver. It's not far. My friend went there and she needs me—please!"

The trapper's mouth opened, and then sadness rushed into his eyes. "I took her there several hours ago. I'm sorry, but she didn't come back."

Amarok closed his eyes, willing the horrible words to evaporate from his mind. He opened them slowly, feeling as if he'd just swallowed a blade.

"I'm sorry," Ben said. "I told her I'd wait an hour and I waited almost two. If she wasn't back by then, she's not coming back." He lowered his dark eyes. "I didn't want to leave her, but I couldn't risk staying. I'm sorry, son, but she had to know going in she wouldn't stand much of a chance against what lives there." The native's eyes strayed to the totems circling Amarok's neck and he smiled sadly, as if his suspicions had been confirmed. "You're brother wolf, aren't you? It was you she was trying to save."

Amarok's knees buckled. He couldn't be too late. It was his job to protect her. The girl he loved couldn't have died giving him a chance at life. Emotions flooded him, choking him with despair.

Ben cleared his throat. "You know the history of that place as well as I do. No one lasts long there."

"But you don't know for sure what happened to her? Not for sure?" Amarok begged, clinging to any shred of hope he could find.

"No. I assumed, when she didn't return, she'd ended up like all the others. No sane person would set foot in the place. It's too dangerous."

"I have to know, either way. Will you give me a ride?"

The trapper held up his hand. "Look, we've already lost one soul. I'm not going to endanger another person. Don't throw your life away, boy. Don't make her sacrifice for nothing."

"But I might be able to save her! If you're not willing to take me, at least let me borrow your boat!"

The man hesitated.

"Ben, please!"

The man nodded. "All right. I warned you, but I suppose there's nobody who knows the dangers better than you. It's your life. Get in."

They traveled downstream, the calm water rippling out from the bow to lap at the nearby banks. The passive section of the river merged with an angry branch and the route stretching before them became a rushing torrent, clogged with snags and dangerous logjams. Amarok clutched the side of the boat and frowned. Over the last century, the river had changed drastically. He thought of Emma and his heart twisted. He would've never sent Emma if he'd known how dangerous it was. He gazed into the belly of the river, remembering the plentiful trout it once provided, how they would burst to the surface on his line, the sizzle of their tender flesh in his mother's frying pan. The memory of the succulent smell of fried fish and pepper permeating the once-cozy cabin caused his stomach to grumble with hunger.

The river branched, and Ben chose the left fork. The color of the water intensified, the aqua blue hue deepening and changing until it turned an ugly brown, heavy with silt. The swells grew taller and deeper in the agitated water. Each wave crested in froths of white claws, scraping at the sides of the boat.

A bird shrieked overhead. Amarok spotted the owl flying low, gliding silently on the winds. With three powerful upstrokes, it sailed across the sky, disappearing into the trees ahead. He breathed a heavy sigh, thankful for his uncle's presence. Over the years, he'd only traveled here a few times as a wolf, and his human perception was so different, it could well have been a different place. Now everything appeared darker, more lifeless.

Even the wind seemed absent, and it struck him how heavy the feeling of death hung over the land.

A tinge of melancholy came over him. He remembered his father's excitement about this unexplored frontier, so untouched by human hands, and he wondered how they'd missed the desolate quality of the region. The land had fooled his parents into trusting it. Even his native mother, who'd always been so perceptive, hadn't recognized what deadly, devious secrets the land held. It had killed her, and then cradled her and her husband in death, roots twisting into their graves to forever hold them prisoner in its rotting, forsaken soil.

A fogbank shrouded the shoulders of the land like a widow's shawl. A mile downriver the haze lifted, and Amarok spotted the sad cabin perched on the rise, and the dilapidated crosses marking the graves. He choked down the lump rising in his throat, feeling as if his gut had been shoveled out with a rusty spade. All the terrible sorrow he'd endured so long ago washed over him anew. His eyes swept across the cold and lonesome graves, the crooked and weather-beaten crosses. So many memories lay buried in the soil with them.

Ben cut the engine and coasted close to shore. Waves slapped the hull, rocking the boat violently. Amarok braced himself and jumped out onto the sandbank.

He glanced over his shoulder at Ben. "I'll be back as soon as I can."

The trapper nodded. "Try not to be too long."

"I'll do my best."

Amarok hurried into the brush, fighting through a maze of alder bushes and overgrown trees. The once-tiny saplings lining the path in his youth now towered toward the sky. Their shadow created a dark and dismal canopy over the lonely trail. Blades of brown grass poked up from snow-encrusted tussocks. Amarok broke through the brush and stood at the front door of the cabin. He'd known every nail, every notch in each hand-hewn log in the structure—now just a dust-covered artifact of dreams destroyed, a family ruined.

He gripped the cold doorknob, closed his eyes, and dropped his hand quickly. He had no time to lament, no time for painful memories. He had to find Emma. Amarok passed the lonely graves with a stab of regret and ducked into the trees.

He wove a shortcut through the tangled undergrowth. The sun poked from behind the clouds, shooting narrow shafts across the earth as if guiding him. Its pale rays shimmered off skiffs of snow jacketing the gray foliage. The sun faded and darkness crept in like a living thing, sucking the life from the land, shrouding it in breathless silence. The quiet rang in Amarok's ears. Inching forward, his eyes shifted back and forth, ears straining to pick up any threatening sound. He skirted the top of the rise, stepping from tree to tree to keep his outline obscured. Carefully, he worked past the base of the mountain and into a stand of trees beyond.

Huddled between two giant pines, the shaman's hut squatted, just as he remembered it. A depressing, dilapidated shack, with smoke billowing from a crude hole cut in the ceiling. The scent of sage and cooked lichens set his instincts on edge. He'd smelled the pungent mixture, boiling in a pot for days, during his transformation. Amarok crept forward, one careful step at a time, as soundless as the fog. He leaned his ear against the door, listening. Nothing. He steeled himself, grabbed the wooden handle and burst inside.

Amarok swept a quick glance around the interior of the smoky hut, on the lookout for the shaman crouching in the shadows.

The walls, blackened by centuries' worth of wood smoke, barely kept the weather out. Packed earth made up a dirt floor, and the circular hole in the thatched roof provided ventilation. All of this was, of course, for his victims. The shaman neither needed shelter or comfort for his immortal shell, but he needed to keep the unfortunate humans alive long enough to complete the transformation. When he was finished, they had nature's protection of fur or feathers and no longer required the meager shelter offered by the ramshackle dwelling.

Amarok's eyes burned from the thick haze of acrid smoke and cooked herbs. Nothing was discernible in the smog. As his eyes struggled to adjust, he saw a cast iron pot hanging over the open firepit, boiling the hateful mixture he remembered so well. He advanced and turned the pot over with a savage kick, extinguishing the flames below. Deeper in the dwelling, he spotted wooden masks and spears carved of bone cluttering the filthy walls. A woolly animal shivered on the floor, near the fire.

Amarok's mouth fell open. *NO!*

37

A strange sound broke into Emma's head; an ancient crackle, reminding her of crinkly old paper. She couldn't quite make out the words, but she continued to shut it out, as well as the unsettling chanting. Whatever she was doing seemed to be working. The burning pain searing her skin had faded. She relaxed, letting herself drift farther and farther away.

Emma ignored the shaman's angry call echoing in some distant place in her mind, filled with rage and hatred, demanding she come back. She drifted to a spot inside of herself that no one could penetrate. This was the place she loved to visit the most, a field filled with daisies behind Grandmother's cottage. She sat with the loving old woman, who had died when she was ten. They laughed and picked flowers, tucking them into each other's hair. Every once in a while, the shaman's angry chant broke through, and she'd look at the vision of her grandmother and smile. Emma forgot all her worries in the woman's soothing gaze.

An itching sensation tickled her nose and arms. Fur brushed against her skin and she sneezed. Somehow, her allergies had broken through into her dream world. Her grandmother smiled and handed her a cup of Earl Gray and a homemade gingersnap. Emma savored the cookie's delicate flavor and sipped her tea, feeling at peace. The scent of animal dander intruded on the serene moment, growing stronger. Her eyes burned, but still she focused on her grandmother's kind face and held her cup out for more tea. She lifted it to her lips, picking out a long strand of fur before taking a sip.

38

Amarok examined the lump of fur resting near the fire. He tiptoed around it, fearing a trap. He viewed it from every available angle before he could finally put a name to the nondescript ball of fluff—a coyote. Small for one of its kind, it was either very young or dwarfed somehow. The creature lifted its head, and then laid it down again, closing its eyes. Amarok's breath hitched in his throat as he crept closer. *Could it be?* The coyote lifted its head again and let out a soft whine. The animal blinked, showing a flash of blue—an extraordinarily rare eye color for a coyote. But they happened to be the same color as Emma's, and its reddish fur matched the shade of her hair. If he touched it, would it be the same silky texture as hers? His throat went dry. He took another step closer, not wanting to believe. The thing fixed pleading eyes on him and whimpered.

Amarok fell to his knees. "Emma, is that you?"

The creature whined again.

"Don't try to move, it's okay. We'll find your totem. I'll fix this, I promise!"

Amarok reached to stroke the coyote, which whined again, this time more pleading, insistent. Amarok choked back tears, leaning closer. The creature suddenly sprang to its feet, growling. Amarok took a step back, then another, as the creature lowered its head. Its eyes filled with rage. Amarok bolted for the door, his unsteady legs slowing him down. He could hear the creature closing in behind him, and then he could hear nothing as the creature sprang into the air.

As he reached the door, the coyote hit him, knocking him flat and driving the air from his lungs, snapping at the back of his neck, its white tongue slithering out like some albino snake as it bit him, hard, on the shoulder. Blood sprayed, and Amarok could feel it coursing down his arm. The creature's muzzle pulled back from its dagger-like teeth as it leaped again. Amarok caught it in both arms, driving him backward. He slammed it to the ground, smashing its small head into the hard-packed dirt. Rewarded with a sickening crunch, Amarok watched as it started to dissolve in his hands, twisting and squirming until it sank into the ground in a heap of hide and bones. Amarok's heart raced. He should have known the coyote was a trap. As a small child, he'd listened while his mother told him tales of tricky coyotes by campfire light, drawing symbols in the ashes, warning him to beware.

Amarok bolted from the hut, scanning the area as he ran. He had to find her. *But where?* His eyes locked on the gaping maw of the cavern in the mountain.

39

Emma smiled at her grandmother through watering eyes. The tickle started far back in her nose, and she slapped a hand to her mouth just in time to catch the explosive sneeze. The old woman handed her a pink hankie, and Emma dabbed at her tearing eyes. Her grandmother smiled, looking down at Emma's lap. Emma realized there was a cat curled up there. She grinned and picked it up, cradling the feline in her arms, despite the price she knew she'd pay. It was Mittens, the long-haired Persian, a treasured companion from her childhood. The cat had always made her sneeze, but she'd loved it and would brave the unpleasant allergic reaction for the sake of an old friend.

Mittens blinked up at her with liquid pools of blue. Emma stroked the cat's fur until it purred, scratching the spots on the cheeks right behind the whiskers and the one between the ears. The animal leaned into her touch, claws kneading painfully into her leg. The purr vibrated loudly, tickling her fingers. She took her furry companion and lay down in the soft field, staring up at the cotton-like clouds. They moved across the sky rapidly, and darker, more threatening ones followed close behind.

A bitter wind seemed at odds with the beautiful day, blowing the dainty lace handkerchief from her hand. Grandma frowned and peered at the sky. She smoothed her knotted hands across her plaid apron and started to pack up their things, tucking them into a basket. Emma sat up, shivering. The sky continued to darken with the gathering storm. Thick clouds muted the bright sunshine, and the faint rumblings of thunder could be heard far in the distance.

Suddenly the sound turned into a tearing shriek, and lightning flashed overhead, illuminating the nearly-black horizon. The skies opened up and heavy droplets of rain splattered their heads. She grabbed for Mittens, but the cat bolted, its claws raking her skin as it leapt from her arms.

"Ouch!" Emma yelled. She tried to pick the cat up again, but it arched its back and hissed. Another flash—followed immediately by a deafening gong of thunder—startled the creature and it ran, disappearing into the tall grass. Emma glanced at her grandmother. The picnic basket still sat on the blanket, but the kindly old lady was gone.

Emma jumped to her feet, whirling around. The field remained—and the tree she'd climbed as a girl—but the house that'd held so many of her happy memories was gone. The field extended into the distance until it met the trees, but not even an impression in the grass showed where, only moments before, an entire house had stood.

Her gaze strayed to the woolen blanket and the one empty teacup remaining. Something about it chilled her and she shivered, spinning again. Fear raked her insides. Something was wrong—very wrong. The scratch on her arm throbbed. As she examined it, she noticed the mist licking at her feet. The ice fog crept in, swallowing everything in its path. It reached her ankles now, climbing higher and higher up her body. The cold burned like fire on her wound and she wrapped her arms around herself.

In the distance, thunder rumbled again, except this time Emma realized it wasn't thunder at all, but the pounding of giant feet. She strained to see into the fog, her throat tight. Exploding through the mist charged a herd of mammoths, their tusks dripping blood, their ebony eyes dead. Emma tried to bolt but the fog slithered around her shoulders, holding her in an iron grip. The mammoths raised their trunks, trumpeting in rage as they drew near. Emma's ears rang as she braced for the terrible collision, but the beasts suddenly swirled into a freezing wall of haze, washing over her, sealing her in a sheet of ice, consuming her.

40

Amarok watched the owl swoop down from the treetops, settling in a thick patch of snow at the foot of the mountain. It beat its wings and gave a soft hoot. Amarok rushed to the bird, spotting Emma's backpack. The owl pulled at the zipper with its black beak.

A chill of dread sank into Amarok's chest like an arrow. He dropped to his knees, unzipped the pack, and spotted a dozen totems jumbled at the bottom. Amarok searched until he found one with an owl and draped it around his uncle's neck. He jumped back as the bird sprang into the air, its big wings slashing toward the cabin, where it swung a hard left and dove inside through one of the broken windows. Amarok waited and watched, holding his breath with anticipation. He'd need Jock's help in dealing with the shaman. There had to be a way to destroy him, but how could he kill someone or something that had survived since the ice age—a creature filled with so much rage and hate it had escaped death for centuries?

Amarok watched the cabin desperately, waiting for what seemed an eternity before the back door swung open, banging in the wind. Amarok's eyes went wide as his breath hitched in his throat. Was it all just a crazy dream? In one swift movement, out stepped the man he'd known so well. His uncle wore a red-checkered woolen shirt, wool pants and mukluks. He lumbered closer, trying to hurry but unsteady on his feet. Amarok charged forward, almost knocking him over, hugging his uncle hard. The big man patted him on the back, and then abruptly pushed him away.

He pinned Amarok with hard eyes. "We don't have much time. He's got the girl. I took the totems from her as Milak dragged her into his lair. I knew the only thing I could do to help her was to try to save you, so you'd be able to come back and rescue her. Now come on, we have to hurry."

They started up the narrow steps leading to the cave and Amarok paused. "After all this time, how did you get free?"

Jock glanced back at him. "I found my totem—the one that freed me—long ago," he said. "But I needed the second one to return to human form. I flew free for decades, but was never crafty enough to find its mate. His magic was much too strong, and I didn't dare come too close for fear he'd ensnare me again, force me to scout for new victims."

They climbed to the ledge, and Jock helped him up. The big man eyed the cave entrance and frowned. "Over time, I hid clothes and supplies I found in your folks' cabin, knowing I would need them someday, never giving up hope. I stuffed them into the burners of your mother's cook-stove, hoping to keep them safe from rodents, and I stored other things as well. I'd almost given up hope, until I watched Suka attack Weasel Tail."

"Do you think now that Weasel Tail is dead, the shaman's powers are weak enough we could defeat him?"

Jock rubbed his square jaw, keeping his eyes fixed on the gloomy entrance. "I don't know, but I think I might know another way." The big man stretched his arms as if his back pained him. "Over the years, I've followed him, searching for my second totem. I never ventured very far into this cave, because if he ever caught me, I'd never be free again. Being a bird had its advantages. I was swifter than most and could hide easily. I noticed that on all the occasions he ventured inside, he never, ever, entered the one tunnel closest to this entrance. From the way he acted, I think there's something in there he's afraid of."

Amarok took a bold step forward. "Good. Now he has even more to fear." He took another step, spotting Emma's flashlight where it had rolled into a crack in the face of the rock. He pried it from its resting spot, and it emitted a weak beam in the afternoon light. Amarok pointed it at the gaping entrance and ducked inside.

Jock grabbed his shoulder. "Give me the light and I'll lead the way. Be careful of sinkholes and traps. Stay at my hip and don't stray. One wrong step, and it might be the death of you."

Amarok nodded and handed Jock the flashlight as they cautiously pressed deeper into the cave. The scent of musk and rancid meat crawled up Amarok's nostrils—the same moldy stench he'd smelled in Milak's hut—a rotting decay penetrating every corner of the cave. A scent he'd never forget. They took an immediate left around a giant sinkhole the size of a small ship and entered a long, skinny tunnel. Bats clung to the ceiling, squeaking in the darkness. Jock put a finger to his lips. "We have to be as quiet as we can. Understand? He can hear every movement we make." Jock pointed up with the flashlight. "And don't disturb the bats; the vile things might be his spies."

They crept farther into the tunnel, crouching to maneuver through its tight corners, until they came to an abrupt dead end. Jock frowned and waved the light around the small chamber. "There has to be a reason he fears this place." He swept the light across the walls to a pile of clear stones. "You know what those are, son?"

Amarok shook his head. "Crystals?"

"Quartz crystals, to be exact, the clear kind that comes in clusters. Quick, gather as many as you can and stuff your pockets full."

"What do you think it will do to him? Can it destroy him?"

Jock set his jaw. "I sure hope so. I've heard stories of the power of crystals from superstitious old sea dogs. The way he never ventured, not even an inch, into this tunnel tells me it's very powerful stuff, indeed. Light always destroys darkness. Just what we need to free the girl."

Amarok's heart jumped. "Thank you, Uncle. It's so good to have you here with me. I thought I had no one left."

Jock patted him on the shoulder. "I never left your side for long. It was hard not being able to help you, to watch so helplessly." He laid a heavy hand on Amarok's shoulder. "You never really know who's looking out for you. Just because you can't always see them with your eyes, doesn't mean they're not there. I believe your father still watches over both of us." He cleared his throat, voice heavy with emotion. "Now," he whispered. "Start picking up those rocks."

They stuffed their pockets full and hurried from the tunnel into the main entrance. Jock cocked his head and listened. "Wait—I hear something."

A terrible chant slithered from the darkness to Amarok's ears. A sound so innately evil, so intolerable, it could not have come from mortal lips. Amarok froze. A ripple of fear shackled his feet to the floor. He recognized the loathsome voice of the shaman, the horrible churning sound of his forked tongue as it clucked against his liver-spotted lips.

"This way!" Jock hissed, waving the flashlight.

Amarok hurried behind his uncle, struggling to keep up, breath sawing in and out, sore body complaining with every step. The chanting grew louder, grating against his nerves, chilling his heart. They worked their way through pools of water and pointed flowstone to yet another winding tunnel, following the dreadful sounds to an enormous cavern. Torchlight flickered, and long, skinny shadows licked the limestone walls. An eerie ice fog clung to every surface, growing denser, colder the farther they crept into the icy room. Amarok shivered, goose bumps broke out across his skin. Frost coated his eyelashes and he blinked to keep them from freezing shut.

Jock held the flashlight high, waving the beam into the darkness. "Look!" He pointed to a massive stone altar. Intricate spirals, arrows, and woolly mammoths ornamented the sides. In the center, Emma lay as if dead. Her lips, a whitewashed pink, curled into a forced smile. Her hair fanned out behind her, the rich red of it in stark contrast to the bluish hue of her skin.

Amarok jolted forward and Jock snatched his arm.

"No, wait!"

Amarok pulled away, impatient to get to Emma. "Why?"

"It's all too easy," Jock whispered.

"What do you mean?"

"The way he just let you waltz across his land, go into his hut, and enter his lair without putting up a single fight." Jock's eyes narrowed. "He's up to something."

"Maybe he's weak?"

"Yes, but he's not stupid, boy."

Amarok nodded. He knew how crafty the shaman was. He grabbed a torch from the wall and raised it above his head to get a better look at the altar where Emma lay. Long, jagged icicles hung from the ends like the satin lining in a coffin.

"I'll go first. Stay behind me," Jock said. "If something happens to me, I want you to get out of here."

"No—I won't leave you, uncle."

"You might have to. No sense in both of us dying."

They worked their way closer. As they came to the side of the stone, Amarok reached to touch Emma, but suddenly the icicles twisted into vipers, striking at his arm. Jock pulled him back. The reptiles dropped from the stone and slithered across the floor at a frightening speed. Their icy hissing echoed strangely in the cavern. Amarok waved the torch at them and they hesitated, drawing back—but only a fraction—before resuming their pursuit. They undulated to his feet, hissing and spitting. He threw the torch to the ground and the ice snakes withered away in the flames.

Amarok rushed to Emma's side. He pulled her into his arms, cradling her body against him. She was so cold, as if he held a block of ice, the chill penetrating into his arms even through his heavy parka.

"Watch out!" Jock yelled.

Amarok caught a glimpse of a figure moving in the fog.

Jock stepped forward, pulling a large crystal from his pocket, aiming it at the dark presence. "Stay back!" Jock warned. He pointed the tip of the stone against the flashlight beam, angling it so the thin shaft of light fractured into a million rays of brilliance. It sent bright color cutting through the fog, seeking out the shadowy figure like diamond spears in the darkness.

The shaman materialized, translucent, staying within the shadows, floating across the stone floor. The darkness didn't hide his leathery, petrified skin and sloping forehead. His eyes, red as the flames of hell, glared with the horrible cunning that Amarok remembered so well.

A paralyzing surge of fear pierced Amarok's heart like a blade. The old man's eyes glittered in triumph.

Jock pulled back his hand to hurl the crystal at him, but an arrow hissed from the fog, zipping through the air to sink deep in between Jock's ribs. The big man fell with a groan, leaning painfully on one elbow, pulling the arrow from his side.

"No!" Amarok screamed. He ran to his uncle's side, laying Emma at his feet and pressing his hand over his uncle's gaping wound. Blood gushed between his fingers.

"I'm okay! Use the crystals," Jock gasped. "Throw them!"

Amarok shoved his hands into his pockets and flung three large crystals into the ice fog. The gems absorbed the almost invisible light, magnifying it. The cavern brightened with their brilliant sparks. A terrible shriek boomed off the walls, shaking the floor. Wind came in a fierce burst, sending bits of shale and sand swirling like shrapnel. It grew stronger, fueled with raw fury, but the shaman didn't appear.

Jock rested against the cave wall, clutching his side. "The crystals keep him trapped!" He struggled to his feet. "It may not last for long."

Amarok scooped Emma up again. "We can seal the entrance to this cave, if we hurry. It won't destroy him, but I bet he won't be able to leave as long as the crystals block the opening!"

"Good plan, boy!"

They ran from the cave, dropping a trail of crystals behind them. Jock clasped his side as he stumbled forward, barely keeping up. "Hurry," he said. "Get out of here, and I'll put the rest of the crystals around the entrance."

Amarok maneuvered down the steps, trying not to bounce Emma too badly. He cradled her to his chest and negotiated the rocky staircase. Watching from the ground, he waited nervously while Jock clambered down the last step.

"Are you sure you're okay, Uncle?"

Jock nodded. "It'll take more than an evil phantom to put an end to Jock! If I die, it'll be at the hands of a jealous husband." He glanced over his shoulder, cradling his side. "We need to keep moving."

They hurried across the open expanse of land, heading toward the moonlit river. Amarok chanced a glance over his shoulder. A glowing mist appeared at the mouth of the cave. The red eyes of the shaman materialized, twin orbs of hatred. His whole outline seemed to glow in the circle of crystals. In one swift movement, a dark mass of angry beasts burst from his leathery chest.

Wolves.

"He's sending dark spirits after us!" Amarok yelled.

Jock wheeled. "Hurry! We have to get some distance between us."

The spirit wolves swirled over the rock face and dropped in a black cloud to the forest floor.

"Head for the cabin!" Amarok yelled.

A stitch jabbed his side, and the muscles in his legs screamed. Even so, he kept running, with Emma in the safety of his arms.

A blood-chilling howl filled the night air behind them. Amarok risked another glance and what he saw froze him clean through. The wolves were gaining on them with terrifying speed, surging over the ground, their crimson eyes wide with bloodlust. From all around came more heart-stopping howls as they called to one another, spreading out, forming a deadly posse.

The wolves swirled around them in the mist. They slowed as they formed a tight circle, herding the three humans in, their saliva-dripping fangs inches from their heels. Two of the ravenous beasts set their blood-colored eyes on Emma, and Amarok vowed to visit Judas in hell before he'd let the wolves have her. They crept closer, carefully. Amarok stared at their lolling red tongues, giant limbs, and razor-like teeth. He knew firsthand what those terrible daggers were capable of.

Jock stepped in front of him, holding out his arms. With a sudden burst, one of the great beasts crashed into Jock with a breath-robbing impact. He kicked it, hard, in the belly. The wolf yelped, and the others turned on Amarok.

A gunshot cracked overhead and Ben emerged from the brush. The wolves whirled and turned on him. He raised the gun to his shoulder and shot the leader dead center in the head. The creature dissolved on impact and the others evaporated to a black cloud of dust.

"Thank God! You saved us." Amarok sank to his knees with Emma.

Ben shrugged. "Never did feel right about chickening out the first time, leaving the girl to begin with. When I heard the commotion from the riverbank, I knew I had to do something."

They hurried through the thick brush to the boat. Amarok's wounds pained him, and his muscles were still so weak, he didn't know how much longer he could carry Emma. In the fray, he hadn't realized how badly his body ached, how tired he was. None of that had mattered, because his only thoughts at the time were of saving her, protecting her. Loving her.

Ben cranked the throttle wide open and they sped across the water. The boat slapped up and down in the choppy current and Amarok wondered if the shaman had something to do with the churning waters.

Amarok sat with Emma, still so lifeless and cold in his arms, while Jock tended to the wound in his side with Ben's first aid kit. Amarok gazed into Emma's ashen face. She appeared even paler in the moonlight. He could feel her faint pulse, but somehow Milak's spell contained enough power to keep her unconscious. Amarok cradled her to his chest, willing all his heat and life spirit to enter into her body, brushing his lips to her cold forehead.

"We better hurry; she doesn't have much time," Jock said. "Looks like hypothermia."

Ben pushed the boat harder, dangerously negotiating the log-jammed path. They sped past the dock at Weasel Tail's cabin and on to the inlet at Ben's place.

Ben cut the engine, jumped from the boat and secured it to the dock. He peered at Emma and shook his head. "I'll take her by plane to the hospital in Eltan. It's the fastest way."

Amarok's heart fell like a stone into a bottomless canyon. He knew it was selfish, he knew it was wrong, but he didn't want Ben to take her from him. To someplace he couldn't go. He never wanted to leave her side again and now, as a man, he had no choice but to let her go.

They hurried up the well-worn path leading to Ben's cabin. "Go inside and stoke the fire," Ben said. "I'll get the plane ready."

Amarok rushed inside and set Emma on the couch by the hearth. He stacked wood in the fireplace, feeding the fading embers. Covering Emma with a thick layer of wool blankets, he stoked the fire high. He sat beside her, his body aching, his heart heavy. He peered out the window, watching Ben and Jock uncover the plane. Ben climbed inside, checking the instrument panel, while Jock unhooked the tie downs. Ben fired up the plane and Jock waved his hands at the window, signaling Amarok to bring Emma.

Amarok hesitated, staring down at the girl he'd protected and come to love. Was this the last time he'd ever see her? His vision blurred, his throat tight with emotion. He wrapped her in the wool blankets, picked her up again and hurried outside.

She looked much paler than when they'd left the cursed lands. Ben held the door open and Amarok's heart sank. How could he let her go alone? He wanted to be at her side to make sure they took good care of her, but the forest still held him prisoner, even as a man. He gazed at her face, memorizing every feature.

He couldn't move. He couldn't let her go. He didn't want Ben to take her from him, but he couldn't stand to watch her die, either.

Jock gripped his shoulder. "You have to let her go, son. It's the only way."

Amarok set her gently in the seat of the plane and buckled her in. A tear splashed onto her cheek as he pressed his lips to hers and kissed her goodbye. He shut the heavy door and stepped back, feeling as if he'd just swallowed a knife. The plane taxied, snow swirling in the air, and took off in a twisting mass of blinding snow.

The nose of the aircraft pulled up, flying higher and higher into the sky. Amarok followed it until it was nothing more than a speck. He clenched his fists until his fingers ached, listening to the lonesome drone growing fainter and fainter, until it disappeared entirely. After everything he'd gone through to hold onto her, he stood helpless, watching her fly miles beyond his reach. He'd wanted so badly to protect her, and now he had to face the one thing he couldn't protect her from—death. Surely, she must be able to feel his love, even across the vast distance separating them. Something so huge, so overpowering couldn't possibly be chained to this single piece of wilderness.

Amarok closed his eyes and focused on sending his loving spirit with her. He visualized it crossing mountains, rivers and over the windy tundra, flowing from him in a brilliant display of energy that would shame the aurora borealis themselves. He fell to his knees, praying to the spirits of his ancestors to spare her.

Amarok sang his songs of mourning and of loss until his throat ached.

He trudged to the cabin, clutching the strap of the backpack. Inside, he pictured the scatter of totems, each one representing a life cut short, a pitiful existence of servitude and misery. He'd find all of their owners and reunite them with their totems; he owed her that much. It seemed a hollow victory without Emma at his side.

Amarok didn't understand the shaman's powers as well as he'd have liked, but he prayed that with the shaman's demise, someday the land would be free. Then maybe, just maybe, the invisible chains holding him captive might finally be broken and he could be with Emma again.

Tears came to his eyes as he recalled the first time he'd felt her hand on his ragged coat, the day he'd made her smile, the feather he'd given her, and the moment he'd protected her from Suka's wrath. He would miss so many things about her. The bitter loneliness of it all ate at his insides.

He wondered if she would ever return here. Amarok looked at Ben's cabin; light glowed from the windowpanes, spilling onto the snow. He saw his uncle standing inside, gazing into the night, waiting for him. Amarok lumbered up the snowy path. Jock would never be able to fill the hole Emma had left in his heart, but at least he no longer had to face life without her alone.

As he neared the cabin, he glanced at the lonely sky. Stars were beginning to twinkle in the early veil of twilight. If Emma died, would he find her among the glimmering specks dotting the heavens? If she passed on, he would die also, and join her in the sky.

41

Emma spotted a black wolf standing on the brow of a snowy hill. It lifted its regal head, watching her with a smoldering gaze. The wolf tipped his head and howled a sorrowful cry.

"Amarok, come!"

The wolf ignored her, pacing the mound. Why wouldn't he come to her?

"Amarok!"

He howled again, a mournful cry that rang across the arctic tundra like the toll of a funeral bell. Emma called him again. Something was wrong. He couldn't hear her. Why was he so sad? She started up the hill, wading through the heavy snowfall. Even with all the clothes she wore, her body was racked with chills. She was so cold, so bone cold.

The wolf circled the mound, digging at the ice-bound soil in frustration. Emma drove herself hard, wading through the snow, her legs so heavy she could hardly lift them, fingers frozen, unable to bend.

Emma almost reached the top of the hill. Icicles clung to her freezing hair. Amarok bayed even louder. Her heart started to pound. What was wrong with him? Was he hurt? Why was he crying like that? Then, as she crested the rise, she saw the answer. Looped around his neck, he wore a heavy collar. The thick, metal chain was secured to a stake driven into the permafrost. She reached to touch him, but her whole arm turned to ice. The freezing then hit her shoulders. Emma tried to move, but the ice crept through her entire body, extending, inches thick, out from her skin.

Emma felt herself lifting into the air, hovering over the frozen soil. Encased like a frozen mummy, wrapped in a solid block of ice. She flew across the land, miles above him, her screams muted in her sub-zero prison. She ached to pound at the ice with her fists. Amarok jumped and pulled at his chains, trying to reach her, howling even louder. Now, she understood his distress.

Her life was in danger, and wherever she was going, he couldn't follow.

42

Days passed like months. Amarok waited impatiently for signs of Ben, returning with news of Emma. Every drone from the sky, every heave of ice on the river, made his heart race. Since her departure, he hadn't been able to think about anything but her welfare and if, someday, she would return to him.

He woke before dawn every morning, hiking the frozen land for any signs of Ben's return. And those lonesome morning walks only added to his feelings of utter isolation. Away from the cabin, there were no human sounds. In fact, there was little to hear of any sounds in the forest during the cold months—only the call of a bird now and then, or the occasional chatter of squirrels, or the rustle of new snow filtering to the ground through frozen pine needles.

A hum broke the silence. Amarok listened intently, putting the rifle, which he unslung whenever he stopped, back over his shoulder. The distant sound grew louder: an aircraft. His heart leapt. The sound faded, and his shoulders drooped. Moments later, it came again, and Amarok stood absolutely still, listening. The humming droned in the distance, growing louder. *Ben!*

Amarok hurried up the trail, his shoulders hunched against the morning chill. His breath came in rapid bursts, forming great white puffs. His raw cheeks tingled with the bitter air. A dry cold had settled over the land, growing meaner by the day, penetrating every layer of his clothing. He had forgotten how much colder he could get as a man without fur, how his lips cracked at the corners and the tender skin of his face burned in the harsh weather.

Amarok headed over a rise and down a deep coulee to emerge near the riverbank. The water ran swift, higher than ever, crowded with pack ice that reminded him of broken eggshells. Soon the water would be cold and frozen like the heart of the shaman. He lumbered up the wooden steps, past Ben's cabin, and to the landing site.

In the distance, he watched the plane drop lower and lower until it touched the ground, rolling to a stop. Streams of swirling snow danced into the air around it, obscuring everything in a white whirlwind. He strained to see Ben's face in the cockpit, hoping for a clue to how Emma might be. The pilot smiled and waved. Amarok's spirits soared. When the engines switched off and the propellers stopped spinning, he ran to greet him.

The cabin door flew open.

"How's Emma?"

Ben pulled off his cap and removed his sunglasses, tucking them into a jacket pocket. "Good. She's still unconscious, but they think she'll pull through. They say it's exhaustion, not any type of internal injury. Her vital signs are getting stronger. They think she'll come around any time now. I'll be returning to the hospital in the morning, and then I'll be back here one last time before the winter on Friday. I should know more, then. And of course, I'll return as usual sometime this spring. I can give her a ride up here then, if she'd like."

"Thank you, Ben. I really appreciate it. She doesn't have any family that I know of. Her mother died in a car wreck and…"

Ben held up his hand. "Someone already spoke to me about it. My wife and I never had any children. Maggie's thrilled to have her for the school year. She has a bed all made up and she's decorating the spare bedroom. Never seen her so excited about anything in all my life." Ben smiled. "It's good to see her so happy."

"That's great news! I really can't thank you enough." Amarok pulled an envelope from his pocket. "Could you give this to her?"

"Sure, I'll drop it off at the nurse's station tomorrow."

Jock came out of the woods, pulling a runner sled loaded with firewood. He saw Ben, waved, and headed over, a big smile on his face. "Thanks for letting us stay here. I'm re-stocking the wood we used. Got pretty cold last night. Looks like we're in for a hard winter." He glanced at Amarok. "We better head over to Weasel Tail's. I'll have a supply list ready the next time you come in, but I'm afraid we can only pay with old gold coins."

"That won't be a problem. Price of gold is up now. I can take your winter trappings in when I come in the spring. That should give you plenty to live on."

"I left some coffee on the stove. Should still be hot, if you'd like some," Jock said. "We'd better be leaving before it gets any later."

"Sure you don't want to stay another night?"

Amarok shook his head. "No, we better get settled in the best we can for winter, take stock of what else we may need, and make sure the place is air-tight."

Ben nodded. "Good plan. The Ryans were a filthy bunch. Best to burn the place down."

"I agree with you, there," Jock said. "The old place is just one bad reminder."

The men said their goodbyes, and Jock and Amarok started the long trek to Weasel Tail's. Amarok inhaled a deep breath and let it out slowly. Gone was the bone-deep worry that'd held him for that excruciating week. And though he knew Emma was recovering, doubt gnawed at him. Why would she return to him? He was an antique, a man from a century ago. Though he'd poured his heart into her letter, the fear wore on him.

43

Emma's eyes popped open. She squinted in the bright fluorescent glow. White walls. White vertical blinds. White floor. The room stood silent, all except for the tubular lighting humming from the ceiling and an annoying bleep somewhere in the distance. She sat up, trying to swallow the dryness in her throat, and the bleeping sound quickened. She was in a hospital bed, tubes leading from her arms under cold metal rails.

The door flew open. A short, heavyset woman with steel-gray hair and a crisp, white uniform walked in.

"Good morning," she said, munching on an apple. "I'm Sally, your nurse. Good to see you awake this morning." She swallowed a bite. "You've really been out of it. Had us all worried." She shook her head and clucked. "It was touch-and-go there for a while."

She grabbed the chart from the end of the bed, rested it against a metal tray, and scribbled a few notes. "How are you feeling?"

Emma rubbed her eyes. "Where am I?"

"Eltan River Hospital."

"What happened? How did I get here?"

"You've suffered hypothermia. A man by the name of Ben Redfeather brought you in here."

Emma threw back her bedcovers. "I have to get out of here." She struggled with the railing.

The nurse held up her hand. "Not so fast, young lady."

"You don't understand. My friend is still out there, and he's hurt."

The nurse paled and shook her head. "Oh, no."

"What is it? What's wrong?"

"We thought you were alone. The man who brought you in here didn't say anything about anyone else."

Emma shook the rails. "I have to get out of here. I don't have time for this. I have to get to him. He needs me."

"Time? I'm sorry, honey, but you've been here over a week. If your friend is out there, it's likely too late."

The words rang in her ears, burned into her brain. No, it couldn't be. She had failed him, and now Amarok was dead, just like her mother. Gone forever. Her heart felt ripped from her chest.

Emma's mouth dropped open, and she started to scream. She screamed until her throat hurt, until they rushed her with a needle. She didn't stop until her eyes rolled back in her head and blessed oblivion chased the horror away.

44

Amarok knelt in the fresh snowfall, his gloved fingers gauging the depth of the huge track. He stood and studied the shrouded landscape. He hoped to find Suka before he went into his den for the winter. Before long they wouldn't be able to find any tracks in the unrelenting flurries. Amarok anguished over freeing the creature. Suka had proved to be a disreputable sort before the transformation, and in the intervening years, insanity had consumed what had remained of the man. His only consolation was that Suka, though undeniably unbalanced, would, as a man, lack the pure destructive capabilities of a full-sized grizzly.

All morning they'd been on the hunt for the bear, searching the most elusive hiding places imaginable—high canyon walls, knolls bound in frozen swamps, and countless other hard-to-reach areas, all to no avail. Although badly wounded, Suka still left traces of carnage in his path—logs ripped to shreds, animals half-eaten, winter caches destroyed. Earlier, he'd spotted crows circling high above, marking a kill. Amarok hiked over a frozen buckle in the landscape. A stiff polar wind rippled the ruff of his fur collar as he wove through a thick growth of alder trees and over clumps of wilted devil's club into an open field. He spotted a wolverine laying on its side with its flank ripped wide open, exposing torn flesh. It seemed the bear wasted more than he ate. Amarok followed the tracks from the kill until he lost the trail.

Even if he didn't find Suka, it helped to occupy his mind. He knew Emma was on the mend, thanks to the update from Ben, but his thoughts continued to wander to what could be... but what likely never would.

Amarok pushed his troubles aside, filling his lungs with chilly air. The frosty morning bit at his exposed cheeks and he squinted against the dazzling light reflecting off the icy surfaces. Amarok knew the dilemma Suka presented had been solved for him, at least for the time being. It was too late in the season to find the bear now.

Jock crested a rise, turned and shook his head, signaling he'd found nothing. Amarok lumbered to his side.

Jock released a heavy sigh. "No sign of him heading south."

"I found a track, but it's not Suka's."

"Well," Jock said, still favoring his wounded side, "we better start back."

Jock led the way, his stride just as wide as Amarok remembered from his boyhood. It felt good to have the big man beside him. Jock made everything seem almost normal, and he filled the aching hole the death of Amarok's parents had left.

Sometimes, when the light was just right, Amarok could see his father in Jock—in the way he moved his hands when he spoke, or how he set his jaw to a challenge, never giving in. In some ways, Amarok had inherited these same traits, as well as his native mother's unbreakable will. Amarok carried his memories like a shrine, keeping those who were gone alive inside of himself. In the dark hours their spirits came to comfort him, and then he sang his songs of mourning.

In the quiet of the evenings, when the bright flames of the hearth burned to silent embers, Amarok and his uncle spoke of many things, but they never discussed the time they'd lost. His uncle seemed content to focus only on the future, although, when the subject turned toward town or the sea, his tone invariably turned wistful and he reluctantly admitted how much he missed it. Sadly, he would never sail again, a prisoner to the same spell that bound Amarok. They could travel only within the boundaries of this great forest, and no farther. If they dared, only death awaited them.

Amarok could only dream of what cities must be like now. He wondered if Emma preferred life in the city, too. The modern world was a mystery to him. He knew about airplanes and pickup trucks, as he'd seen them here in his refuge. He'd seen snowmobiles and four-wheelers, too. And Amarok had heard hunters speak of telephones, computers, and iPods as they passed briefly through his limited range, but he couldn't even imagine what such things were. In his time, life was simpler, and the loss of it pained him greatly. If ever he walked among men again, the adjustment might prove difficult.

Before Emma, he could have learned to cope with the utter solitude of his life now, with only his uncle's company. But with her entry into his life, everything had changed. She'd awoken the flames of his soul and only her presence would keep the fire burning within him. He watched the snow tumble endlessly from the sky to rest in clumps on the ground, and spring seemed an eternity away.

He set his mind on survival, knowing they'd need shelter for the winter. Neither he or Jock could stand the thought of settling in Weasel Tail's former home. For Amarok, it held far too many memories of the days he'd spent there as both prisoner and wolf. And for Jock, it was a reminder of how he'd failed to help his nephew for so many years.

They'd agreed to build a new cabin, staying at Weasel Tail's only until the construction could be completed. The new dwelling would be a twin to the one Amarok had built with his father, but far from the shaman's reach.

As they headed home, discussing what supplies they'd need for their new project, a badger exploded from a stand of willow shrubs. It ran at them, and then stopped a foot away. Stomping its thick legs, it stared at them and grunted.

"Well, now." Jock eyed the creature with one cocked brow. "Isn't that a curious thing?"

Amarok studied the animal. *What did it want?* "Look!" he yelled. "It has a totem!"

Jock grinned. "So it does."

Amarok dropped the pack and fell to his knees in the snow, digging through the bag. Opening the lower compartment, he sorted through the totems Emma had liberated, examining each one.

The badger growled and pawed at the snow again. Amarok took another look at the short-legged creature, with its bristly coat of silver-gray, a black and white mask on its broad face, with white margins on its stubby ears. Amarok frowned—none of the totems looked anything like the animal. Then, he spotted one half-hidden in the bottom of the bag, faded with age and chipped on the side. The creature crept forward, nose twitching. Amarok held up the totem to make sure the animal saw it. He approached very slowly, so as not to frighten it. Rather than being nervous, the badger charged, sliding to a stop at Amarok's feet.

Jock raised his gun. "Be careful, boy!"

Amarok knelt, draping the totem around the creature's neck where it clacked gently against its mate. He jumped back and watched in sympathetic fascination as the poor creature made the painful transformation back to human. As his fur disappeared, Amarok dug into the pack again, pulling out the elk hide he carried in case he got trapped away from the cabin, and draped it over the transforming creature, for both warmth and. modesty. In a matter of moments, a wrinkled old man stood before them. Instead of smiling with joy, the man scowled, shaking his fist.

"It can't be," Jock said.

"Do you know him?"

The man glared at them with hard, raisin-like eyes. He gritted his teeth and snarled something that Amarok couldn't understand.

"I'm sorry," Jock said. "I never meant you any harm."

Clutching the hide around himself, the man opened his mouth, spewing a slur of foreign words, lunged forward, and rammed his bald head into Jock's stomach. The wind whooshed from the big man's lungs as his attacker scrambled to his feet. He kicked at Jock, and Amarok tackled him. The little bald man flung him aside, screaming like a madman, and then jumped to his feet and retreated into the brush.

Jock slammed his fist into the snow. "Dammit!"

Amarok got to his feet and offered Jock a hand up. "Are you all right, Uncle?"

Jock stood, tore his stocking cap off his head, and slapped it against his knee.

"Uncle Jock, what's wrong?"

Jock's big shoulders sagged as if carrying a thousand-pound bag of sand. "It's all my fault," he muttered.

"What do you mean?" Amarok asked, studying his uncle's face. "You didn't have anything to do with all this."

Jock shook his head, and set his gaze on the setting sun. "Yes, unfortunately, I did."

45

Emma woke to a brutal throbbing in the base of her skull. Every movement made her head swim. She sat up, clutching her neck to stop the pain. Across from her, perched in a plastic chair, a man scribbled in a notebook. His legs were crossed and his polyester suit looked decades out-of-date. He remained immobile, stoic, watching her every movement. Judging her. She knew who he was without even asking. Her screaming had brought a shrink. She knew all the things he'd say before he even opened his mouth.

He cleared his throat and smiled. "Hello Emma, my name is Dr. Reynolds. I'm a therapist here at the hospital."

He flashed his name-tag, still smiling. Emma spotted what looked like spinach stuck between his front teeth. She knew the game, and she also knew she had to be careful. No matter what happened, she couldn't let him know she was a minor alone. It would be a one-way ticket to a foster home, and then she'd never know what had happened to Amarok.

"Glad you're awake. You gave us all quite a scare."

Emma looked at the wall, wishing he'd just go away.

"How are you feeling now?"

"Okay, I guess."

"I'm here to see if there is anything you'd like to share with me. Any issues that I might be able to assist you with?"

"Issues?"

"The nurse told me that when you were admitted, she saw scars on your arms. Would you like to share with me how long this has been going on?"

Emma's stomach fell. *Great, here we go again.*

"I don't know what you're talking about."

Dr. Reynolds frowned and leaned back in his chair. "You know, it's nothing to be ashamed of. Cutting behaviors are somewhat common among young women in your age group. Perhaps while you're recovering, you'd like to discuss other avenues of release to rid yourself of these self-harming urges."

Emma shook her head. "That was something from my past. I don't cut anymore."

"So the scars are old ones, then? No recent thoughts of harming yourself?"

"Yes and no. I don't even think about it anymore."

"Well," he said. "Then that's good news. But, if ever it gets to be a problem again, you will seek help, right?"

Emma nodded.

"Would you like to tell me what happened?" He glanced at his watch. "I mean, how you ended up in this present condition."

Emma sighed. Here it was, the game—like chess, but the pieces were bits of information. She'd have to think moves ahead to avoid letting him trap her, because checkmate would mean not only her freedom, but likely Amarok's life. Her heart twisted. *If he's still alive.* What good old Dr. Reynolds didn't realize was that she'd played this many times before, and she'd gotten very good at it. He wanted her to spill her guts, and then he could check out in time for an early dinner with his wife. He'd never believe the fantastic things that had happened to her; he *wanted* a cut-and-dry answer. That was exactly what she'd give him.

"I just got lost. That's all."

"Lost? Are you sure?"

Emma nodded and pain darted behind her eyes.

"The nurses had to give you an injection. They said you were hysterical, screaming one certain word or name." He glanced at his tablet. "Amarok?"

The sound of Amarok's name on the man's lips brought tears to Emma's eyes. She couldn't allow herself to cry, and she couldn't let him know about Amarok, either. She wanted to protect his memory—keep it safe, and all to herself.

"It was my brother's name. He died when I was nine. Guess I was just having a flashback or something."

"So, you were alone, then? We don't have to worry about trying to find anyone else?"

"No, I was alone."

The shrink took a toothpick from his pocket and stuck it into his mouth. Emma stared at the piece of spinach still wedged between his front teeth.

"We have some therapeutic art classes that I feel would be beneficial to you, if you'd be willing to participate."

"No thanks. I can't even draw stick figures and besides, I won't be staying that long."

"You'll be here at least another two days. They want to keep a close eye on you. You were in serious shape when you were brought in here." He stood, and Emma couldn't help but notice a smile tugging at the corners of his lips. "Here's my card, in case you need anything," he said, offering her a plain, white business card.

"Thanks."

He took one step out of the room, paused, and then came back in and shut the door. "I almost forgot. There's one more thing I need to mention. You see, while you were out of it, the Sheriff matched your description to the driver's license he found in your car. Since you're a minor, we had to contact your stepfather."

Emma opened her mouth to protest, but Dr. Reynolds continued. "He informed us he has no guardianship rights and provided us with the name of your father."

"My father? I don't have a father."

"I spoke with him yesterday." His voice trailed off as he dropped his gaze to the floor. "He made it clear he didn't have any parental rights either, and to be frank, he sounded..."

"Uninterested? Mad that you were bugging him? That sounds like my dad, all right."

"No, actually quite the opposite. He sounded very concerned about you, but unfortunately he's incarcerated in Texas. He didn't want you to know."

"Incarcerated? You mean, like prison?"

"I'm afraid so, Emma. And that leaves us with no choice but to seek foster care."

Emma's brain spun in a thousand directions. Where would they send her? How would she ever get back to Amarok? Even if he'd died, she still wanted to return to find out for sure. She'd promised him before she left that, no matter what happened, she'd return.

"No, no way! I'm not going to live with strangers."

He held up his hand. Emma spotted a flimsy gold band circling a pale finger.

"Now, listen, I may have good news. Luckily enough for you," the shrink said, "the gentleman who brought you here offered to take you in. His family is well known here. I think they would make a suitable home for you, for the school year at least. And if it doesn't work out, we can make other arrangements. What do you think?"

Emma released a sigh. She could stay with Ben, and he'd be able to take her back to the mountains, back to Amarok. "Okay, that would be cool."

"Good, then it's settled. I'll phone the family and make the arrangements."

The doctor stepped from the room and Emma laid her aching head on the pillow. Before she could close her eyes, he ducked back into the room.

"I'm sorry; I almost forgot. I have a letter for you."

Emma's chest tightened. *Was it bad news? Good news? Would she go crazy if it was from Ben, telling her of Amarok's death?* A thousand disturbing thoughts battered her exhausted mind.

46

Jock walked a few feet away and sat on a stump. He glanced at Amarok, and then lowered his eyes. "Yes, that's true. I'm not the cause of all of this, but I am the cause of that man's entrapment."

Amarok frowned. "But, how?"

"It's a long, sad story. One I haven't thought of in quite some time." The big man folded his arms across his chest. "The guilt of it forced it to the darkest places of my mind. Through the years, it would resurface and the feelings of regret would tug at my heart again." Jock plowed his hands through his hair and slipped on his stocking cap. "When I came from the coast to fetch you for our fishing trip, I couldn't get anyone to bring me here. No one would come within ten miles of this place. I laughed it off. I couldn't believe that anyone could be more superstitious than sailors, but I was wrong. No one was willing to help."

Amarok shrugged. "That doesn't surprise me. The locals all knew better."

Jock nodded. "I met a man in town, at the Klondike Saloon—the man you just saw. His name was Eska. He spoke very little English, but from what I could gather, he was working a mine, raising a large family, and trapping upriver—not far from the valley where you lived. The saloonkeeper told me that Eska would do anything to support his family. He said Eska's wife, who was much younger than he was, had been ill with tuberculosis and unable to care for their children. Because of her grave condition, he had little time to hunt or work his mine."

"But, you had no idea that the curse was real. Only a fool would believe such tales."

Jock's face paled. His eyes softened and he rubbed the whiskers covering his chin. "But I took advantage of his desperate situation." Jock slammed a fist into his thigh. "Eska begged to drop me off a mile from the cabin, and I refused. He told me his children needed him. That it was too risky. And I told him that I wouldn't pay him unless he dropped me off right at the riverbank, right in front of the cabin. I knew he wouldn't refuse because he needed the money. At the time, I didn't believe in the nonsense he was telling me. I should've listened and agreed to his wishes. I never should've pushed him."

Jock's gaze dropped to the ground, his face filled with sadness. "Just a half a mile from the shore our boat capsized, even though there was no wind. When I awoke, unable to move, I saw Eska pleading with the shaman, begging that vile creature not to take him, as his family would surely perish." Jock swallowed hard. "That evil monster turned a blind eye and deaf ear to him, taking even greater pleasure in his suffering. I can still hear Eska's cries as he changed from man to beast. Trapped forever, knowing that his wife and young children would starve to death."

Amarok stared at the spot in the brush where the angry man had vanished, trying to push the haunting sounds of children's hungry cries from his mind.

"You had no way of knowing any of this would happen. Don't be so hard on yourself, uncle."

"I know that, son, but he tried to tell me, and I pushed him into it. I put us both in danger, being so damn insistent and bullheaded. If he could've dropped me off upriver, he would've been home that night, tending to his ailing wife and children."

"Where do you think he's going?"

"Downriver, I imagine, where he lived before all this happened." Jock rubbed his chin and frowned. "To a home, rotting into the earth, and his family resting in cold graves."

Amarok shivered. "At least he's free now."

"But the life he once had is gone. You know it as well as I do. Once it's gone, you can never recover those lost years."

Amarok had no answer, since his uncle was right.

"Well," Jock said. "We have a lot more people to find and to free, by the number of totems you're carrying in that pack."

"I don't think reuniting the others will be so easy," Amarok said. "I can't imagine that very many have found their original totems. Weasel Tail kept them well hidden."

"We'll find them, no matter where that degenerate hid them. Even if we have to rip the place apart." Jock eyed the sky. "Better head home before it gets any later."

Neither of them wore a watch, still measuring time by the progress of the sun floating lazily over the edge of the horizon.

"We'll take stock of the supplies we'll need for the winter." Jock glanced at Amarok and winked. "Hope you're a good cook."

"Sorry," Amarok said. "But if I'm doing the cooking, we'll be skinny by spring."

The big man laughed and slapped him on the shoulder.

A plane buzzed overhead. Amarok's heart leapt. Jock turned to him with a grin and the two men doubled their pace for Ben's.

47

Dr. Reynolds reached into his coat pocket and held out a sealed envelope. Emma saw her name written neatly, in old-fashioned print, across the front. She reached for it, and he snatched it away.

"Not so fast," he said with a smile. "We have a few things to discuss before I give you this." He tapped the letter against the palm of his hand a few times.

Emma frowned, her temper flaring. She didn't have time for games. "What do you mean? It's mine, isn't it?"

"Yes, of course, but first I want a promise from you."

"What kind of promise?"

He paused and gave her a stern look. "That if I give you this letter, you won't try to get out of bed again, young lady. Not until you're better. You need your rest. It's very important to your recovery."

"Okay, I promise." Emma gave him a frosty glare and held up three fingers. "Scout's honor. Now can I have my letter?"

He grinned and slapped the envelope into the palm of her hand. He turned before leaving. "I'll be here if you decide you need to talk to someone."

"Thanks." Emma glanced at him, then at the wall, wishing he would just leave so she could open it in private.

He turned on his heel and headed into the hallway. Emma leaned over the side of her bed, peering into the busy foyer. She watched him saunter to the coffee machine and rummage in his pocket. He dropped some coins into the vending machine and pulled out a giant-sized cup. Taking a sip, he disappeared around a corner. Confident he was truly gone, Emma examined the envelope. She had so many unanswered questions. Maybe the answers were all here in this letter. Emma held her breath, her hands shaking. *Please, be good news.* She tore open the envelope.

Dearest Emma,

I have so much to share with you. But first, I want you to know, I wish with all my being that I could be at your side. The curse will not allow me to leave the walls of the forest. And so with a heavy heart I must tell you that I'm afraid many months will pass until we are able to see each other. Thankfully, Ben has been checking on you, and with each day the doctors say you are getting stronger. I am so grateful.

I hope and pray that you will return with Ben in the spring and join me here next summer. During this dark chapter of separation, I will spend the winter helping those your bravery has helped to set free. Until then, I'll be waiting for you and missing you.

Amarok

Emma pressed the letter to her lips. She closed her eyes and breathed deeply, inhaling the traces of his scent that clung to the paper. Joy surged in her and threatened to bubble over. Amarok was alive! Somehow, he'd gotten his totems. Emma glanced out the hospital window at the white landscape, a strange mirror-image of the barren, white hospital. A thick layer of frost sparkled across fresh mounds of snow, glimmering in the sunlight. Icicles hung like sculpted crystal from sagging tree limbs. So much snow had fallen while she'd been asleep. And so many changes had occurred since she'd fled from home that dark night. She leaned her head on the pillow and gazed into the mountains where she knew Amarok waited, as loyal and patient as ever. Emma smiled and her thoughts turned to spring.

The End

A cruise ship.
A beautiful island.
Two sexy guys.

What could possibly go wrong?

In the Bermuda Triangle—a lot.

Triangles

Kimberly Ann Miller

Coming in June 2013

January 2013

Having poison running through your veins and a kiss that kills really puts a dent in high school.

Kelly Hashway

Touch of Death